FRANKLY, FRANNIE

Books 1-3

D0123809

GROSSET & DUNLAP
Published by the Penguin Group
Penguin Group (USA) LLC, 375 Hudson Street, New York, New York 10014, USA

USA | Canada | UK | Ireland | Australia | New Zealand | India | South Africa | China

penguin.com
A Penguin Random House Company

The Library of Congress has cataloged the individual books under the following Control Numbers:
2009037776, 2009053389, 2010014757.

ISBN 978-0-448-48461-7   10 9 8 7 6 5 4 3 2 1

FRANKLY, FRANNIE

Books 1-3

by AJ Stern • illustrated by Doreen Mulryan Marts

Grosset & Dunlap
An Imprint of Penguin Group (USA) LLC

To Julie Barer, my deus ex machina.—AJS

Thanks go to Lili Stern for her hot pink edits
and Frannie-like qualities, Francesco Sedita,
Bonnie Bader, Caroline Sun, Christine Duplessis,
Jordan Hamessley, Scottie Bowditch, Kimberly
Lauber, Meagan Bennett, and everyone at Penguin
for their support and enthusiasm. Huge thanks to
Doreen Mulryan Marts for drawing Frannie just how
I imagined her. To Julie Barer and William Boggess
and also to my friends and family for their endless
support. A monumental thanks, of course,
and especially, to Judy Goldschmidt for calling
me to ask if I had any ideas.—AJS

FRANKLY, FRANNIE

by AJ Stern • illustrated by Doreen Mulryan Marts

CHAPTER

"I have simply magnificent news!" Mrs. Pellington called from the front of the room.

We had just come back from gym class and we were still feeling run-aroundy, so Mrs. P. gave two long claps followed by three fast ones. This is our signal to clap back and concentrate.

I love clapping back songs. If there are jobs other than teaching where you get to song-clap, I want to work at one.

Mrs. P. always announces **"simply magnificent news"** on Thursdays. Mostly it's about school things like changes on the chore calendar or cleaning out the gerbil cage. But today, Elizabeth Sanders's dad was standing next to Mrs. P., which meant that maybe the news really *was* **simply magnificent**.

Elizabeth's dad is very important and interesting. **It is a scientific fact that he has his own radio show**. And if he has a radio show, then he must have an office. And if you don't already know this about me, **I love offices**.

If Mr. Sanders has an office, then he probably has an assistant. Which is the exact thing I told my parents I wanted for Christmas.

They're thinking about it.

Mrs. P. was so excited that she didn't wait long to blurt out, "Mr. Sanders has invited our class to visit his radio station on Election Day!" Then she covered her heart with both hands and gave Mr. Sanders big, blinky cartoon eyes.

Our whole class sucked in a fast gulp of happiness. Elizabeth acted like it was no big deal. But she only did this because Mr. Sanders is her dad. Secretly she was proud. I could see a really small smile on her face. I'm very smart about really small smiles.

Mr. Sanders's show is about news. My parents listen to *The Sandy Sanders Show* every morning. I am not supposed to say this in public, but my parents think that he is good at some things and not so good at others. A for instance of what I mean is that he's good at the news part, but not at the call-in part. Sometimes my parents slap their heads at his advice and say, "What on earth is he talking about?"

"Isn't this fabulous? Aren't we lucky?! We'll see firsthand how a radio station works," Mrs. P. said. Then she looked right at me and changed her face channel to strict.

"There will be special conditions for certain people."

That was when my whole body started to turn hot. This is because of what happened on the last class trip.

We went to the office of *Cambridge Magazine,* and the office man let us all take turns in his swivel chair. We could swivel all we wanted, but we weren't to touch anything on his desk. But my dad says a messy desk is the sign of a messy mind. Maybe the office man didn't know this because his desk was very messy. When it was my turn in the chair, **I got a great idea**. And that idea was that when the office man's back was turned, I would surprise him by quickly organizing his papers.

But not everything went according to plan. When I reached over to straighten the papers, I knocked over a glass, which spilled water all over his desk. The office man was very upset. He kept squeezing his hands together saying the papers were "originals." My dad calls me an original, which is a good thing. So I didn't understand why the office man was so upset. Or why I got in such big trouble. Now I know. **Original means one of a kind.** Which is good if you're a person, but bad if you're wet paper.

"Does anyone have any questions for me?" Mr. Sanders asked.

My hand shot up so tall, I felt like I could have touched the ceiling without a ladder. Everyone else's hands shot up, too. When he chose me first, I knew I had a really lucky arm.

"Actually, Mr. Sanders, does a radio station have an office?" **Actually** is a really grown-up word and I like to use grown-up words as oftenly as possible.

"Yes, actually, we have a lot of offices."

See what I mean about **actually**?

"How many offices?" I asked.

"Everyone who works there has an office. And there are more than twenty people who work there."

More than *twenty* offices!? In one

place!? A veterinarian only had one office. A dentist sometimes had three. But twenty? They probably had a lot of staplers.

"But the most exciting office is the big one in the middle."

"Why?" I wanted to know.

"That's where all the action is. That's where all the disc jockeys work."

I raised my hand one more time.

"Yes, again?"

"How old do you have to be to work actually at a radio station?"

"Well, actually, some of our interns are as young as eighteen years old."

Eighteen? That was in **twenty-sixteen years**! I did not want to wait that long for a job.

At the end of the day, Mrs. P. gave us permission slips to take home.

But she pulled me aside. "Please ask your parents to come speak with me at school."

That is not such a good sentence. And that is a **scientific fact**.

CHAPTER

When I got home, I slammed the front door behind me so everyone would know I was there. At school they get mad when you do that.

"Frannie? That you?" my mom called from upstairs.

Frannie.

What kind of a name is that, anyway? It sounds too much like fanny, which is another word for butt. And butt is not such a nice word.

Frankly, I don't understand why kids can't just name themselves. **(Frankly! Now there's a good name!)**

"My name is *Frankly*!" I yelled, pulling open the refrigerator with both hands.

"Frankly, that you?" my mom called again. I changed my name a lot. My parents were used to it. Sometimes I added titles, like Doctor or Mrs., because they were really grown-up. "YES!" I shouted back, as I stuck my head in the refrigerator.

I pulled out some bread, a package of sliced turkey, mustard, and lettuce. **I am the only kid I know who likes mustard.**

Okay, here's a secret. I don't really like mustard. It's too spicy, but I like the *idea* of liking mustard. Every grown-up I know likes mustard and I want to do grown-up things.

I opened the lid on the mustard and sniffed. It made the inside of my nose crinkle. I quickly put the lid back on. I try to smell it as **oftenly** as I can. My dad says you can't be good at something without practice. So, I practice liking mustard. Ketchup isn't grown-up at all.

I held my sandwich in one hand, skimmed the wall with my other, and climbed the stairs to my parents' room on the second floor.

My mother was lying on the bed, reading the newspaper.

"Hi, button!" My mom's cheeks looked rosy. That's how they look when she's sick. My stomach flumped over.

I do not like when my mom is sick.

I felt tears welling up in my eyes. "You seemed okay when you drove me to school . . . And now you're in bed. Are you sick?"

It is a **scientific fact** that my mom drives me to school and that my best friend Elliott's mom drives me home. And Elliott, too, of course!

My mom smiled and scooted closer, wrapping me up in her arms. **I** love my mother **so so so so** much. She nuzzled my neck and kissed me all over my cheeks until her powdery smell rubbed off on me.

"No, Lovey Dove, I'm not sick."

I wanted to believe her, but she paused for too long before answering. **I**'m very smart about pauses. So maybe she wasn't telling the truth.

I put down my sandwich and ran
to the bathroom as she called out,
"Where are you going?"

"To get you some tissues."

When I returned, I held them to her
nose and said, "Blow."

My mother laughed and gently
lowered my arm. "I'm not sick, Lovey."

I ran back to the bathroom to get a
thermometer and put it in her mouth,
even though I didn't know how long
to keep it there. I tapped my foot
a couple times and looked at my
wrist even though I did not wear
a watch. Finally, it was boring, so
I pulled the thermometer out of her
mouth.

"Do you feel better now?" I asked.

"Lots," she said. "Now do you
believe that I'm not sick?"

I picked my sandwich back up, shrugged, and with my mouth full, said, "I guess so."

"I know you're concerned, but I'm really fine. I just took a personal day."

"What's a personal day?"

"Sometimes people don't go to work because they're on vacation and sometimes people don't go to work because they're sick, but there's another kind of not going to work and that's called a personal day. When you take the day off because you have a lot of personal business to take care of."

This gave me an idea.

"Can I take a personal day?"

I could tell my mother thought this was hilarious because she laughed so hard, her eyes watered. Then she said, "Oh, Frannie, you are such a comedian." But I don't want to be a comedian. Comedians don't have offices.

"I'm not sure schools give out personal days," she said.

"Well, that's not very fair. Kids should be allowed the exact same things adults are allowed."

"You think adults have it pretty easy, don't you?"

"Yes, I do. Kids have it much harder." *Especially when they have to tell their parents Mrs. P. wants to talk with them.*

"It's not so easy for us, either, you know," said my mother.

I shrugged. I didn't believe her. She said things like this all the time just to make me feel better about not being older.

A while later the front door opened, and we heard my dad singing along to his iPod. He's a really bad singer. Sometimes my mom and I cover our ears to joke with him.

19

I hopped off the bed and ran down the stairs.

"There's my Bird!" my dad called. I jumped up for a lift-hug. My dad is the only person who calls me Bird. It is a **scientific fact** that Bird is my middle name. **But please, do not tell anyone.**

"What's new with today?" he asked.

"I was mom's doctor and I fixed her, because I'm really good at that job. And I changed my name."

"What's your new name?" asked Dad.

I took a very long breath and then announced, "My name is now Frankly!" I looked down at all the mail in my father's hand. Opening mail was really grown-up.

My dad looked up at the ceiling for a minute, then back down at me.

"Frankly. I like it."

Then my mom came down and we all went into the kitchen and I helped make dinner. Some families say grace or a prayer before their meals, but not my family. My family says, **"To the Millers!"** because that is our last name.

After we said "To the Millers!" we talked about the news of the day. My parents like to talk about politics. I have very strong opinions about politics. And my opinions are that **politics are boring**.

"I have something to say."

"Well, we'd love to hear it," my dad said.

He and my mom both leaned back in their chairs. I had their full attention.

"My class is going to visit *The*

Sandy Sanders Show. At an actual real-life radio station."

"Uh-oh," was what my mother said.

My father inched his way forward to the edge of his seat. "Hmmm . . . What did Mrs. Pellington have to say?"

That was the exact question I did not want to answer.

I answered it, anyway. "She wants to have a talk with you."

My dad folded his arms across his chest. "Yeah, she probably wants us to have a good long talk about the *Cambridge Magazine* trip and your curious hands."

"That was a long time ago. My hands are really different now!"

"Birdy, it was three weeks ago!"

"But I know better now! I won't touch anybody's desk. I promise."

I realized that I needed to be very serious. So I thought for a minute. The only way to show them how serious was to use my English accent. I spoke very slowly, just like Eliza Doolittle in *My Fair Lady*.

"It is a scien-tific faakt that I will nawt touch any-theng."

My parents looked at each other. They sent tricky smiles back and forth.

My dad said, "We'll see what rules Mrs. Pellington suggests."

My mom looked me directly in the eyeballs. "And you will have to follow them."

I flumped my hands to my side. I really hoped Mrs. P. was in a **simply magnificent** mood.

CHAPTER

When I woke up the next morning,
I had a hurricane of butterflies in my
belly. That's what happens when I
get nervous. My best friend, Elliott,
gets moths. It's a **scientific fact** that
butterflies are big and moths are
small. He says he can feel a **machillion**
wings in there, and there's no way a
machillion butterflies would be able to fit
in his stomach. So they've got to be moths.

My mom was downstairs drinking

her coffee. I was trying to be very silent. If my mother didn't hear me, maybe she'd forget about me and then maybe she would forget to take me to school.

But before I even knew it, we were in the car. And before I even knew it again, we were already in the school parking lot. When we drove around to find a parking space, there were a lot of trucks. And coming out of the trucks were people carrying big booths. I guess I forgot about being silent because my mouth blurted out, "What are they doing?"

"They're carrying in the voting booths to get ready for next Tuesday."

"We're getting a new president?"

"No, it's time for a new mayor. Didn't Mrs. Pellington tell you?"

I shook my head no. But a little voice in my brain wasn't as sure. "Did she?" it asked.

"Chester Elementary is where the entire east side of town will vote for the mayor on Tuesday."

My mouth almost dropped off my face. My school was going to be one big voting office for the entire east side of town!

"That is actually really important," I said.

"It certainly is," said my mother. Certainly is also very adult-sounding.

As my mom and I climbed up the stairs toward my classroom, I concentrated hard on sending a wish from my heart into her brain. The wish was: I wish you would forget all about your meeting with Mrs. Pellington! But it didn't work.

Mrs. Pellington was waiting at the top of the stairs. I thought if I stood there with both of them, it would stop them from talking about me, but that didn't work, either, because Mrs. Pellington said, "Frannie, why don't you go inside the classroom and give me and your mother one minute alone?"

I will actually tell you for a **scientific fact** that it was **absolutely**, **positively**, and **certainly** not just one minute. I know this because I counted. My entire class and I watched through the window on the classroom door as my mom and Mrs. Pellington talked. Then Elliott did armpit farts. All the kids laughed at this. I made my mouth laugh with the rest of the kids. I even acted out laugh noises, but my insides did not think it was funny at all.

I was too nervous about what my mom and Mrs. P. were **actually** saying to each other. I wanted to hear them but I couldn't.

I did hear someone shout, "Watch out, Millicent!" though. I turned around right as Millicent banged into Will. Millicent loved to read so much that anytime Mrs. P. turned her back, Millicent pulled out a book. Her hands were so fast that by the time Mrs. P. turned back again, Millicent's book was already hidden and she wore her "I'm paying the best attention of anyone" face.

When I turned back, my mom and Mrs. Pellington were shaking hands. Then my mom turned to wave to me and left.

As Mrs. Pellington walked back into the room, her face was very in-charge-ish. Almost like she was the mayor herself.

"Let's step outside the classroom and talk for a second," she whispered in my ear. I had a **maybe I'm not getting ANY presents for Christmas** feeling as I followed her out. What if I wasn't allowed to go on the trip? What if I had to sit in the classroom all by myself and wait **twenty-eighteen hours** for everyone to come back?

Mrs. Pellington cleared her throat. "Your mother and I talked and we decided that we will allow you to join the class on this trip."

I let out a sigh the size of the Grand Canyon.

"But . . ." added Mrs. P.

"I will be assigning special buddies for this trip."

And that's when I knew exactly where the no Christmas presents feeling was coming from.

CHAPTER 4

"Class, I will be assigning special buddies for this upcoming Tuesday's class trip," announced Mrs. P. when we got back to the classroom.

The best part about buddies is that we always get to choose our own. Elliott is always mine and I am always his. I knew how sad Elliott would be when he found out we would not be buddies this time. But before I could send him a note about it through my brainwaves,

Mrs. P. was already saying, "Millicent will be Frannie's buddy."

Millicent looked up and smiled at Mrs. P. in a very official way even though she secretly had a book on her lap and was not being official at all.

I could see all of Elliott's hopes pour through his body and drip onto the floor in a big disappointment puddle. If Millicent was truly a special buddy, then maybe on Tuesday she would let me switch her for Elliott.

Mrs. P. said she wanted to tell us a very good and funny story. I love stories, and Mrs. P.'s are good because she tells us about what life was like in the olden times, when she was a kid.

I leaned forward to make sure not to miss anything. That was the exact moment that Elliott gave a note to

Sarah who gave it to Aaron who gave it to Elizabeth who gave it to Sasha who gave it to me. That was also the moment Millicent took her book back out and started reading again.

I love getting notes in class, even though it is against the law. I opened it up on my lap so Mrs. Pellington wouldn't see.

Elliott had drawn a picture of himself frowning. The word BUDDY was written on top, and under the drawing his own name was crossed out. It gave me a sad feeling. I had to be very careful about sending a note because if I got caught, Mrs. P. might give me *two* "special buddies."

I drew a picture of myself and wrote, "Frankly Boredy Miller," which is a joke about being bored and also about my middle name. (Elliott is the only person who's not in my family who knows my middle name.) Then Elliott sent another note and I wrote him back again. Millicent squinched her face at me. She was getting the "Frannie's special buddy" job confused with the "Frannie's boss" job.

I looked right into Elliott's eyes and sent a note to his brain. It said, "We should probably pay attention now." I know he got it because we both turned to the front of the class to listen to Mrs. P.

". . . the election has been moved from our school to the local theater!" she said. I must have missed the end of her story because now she was talking about the election again.

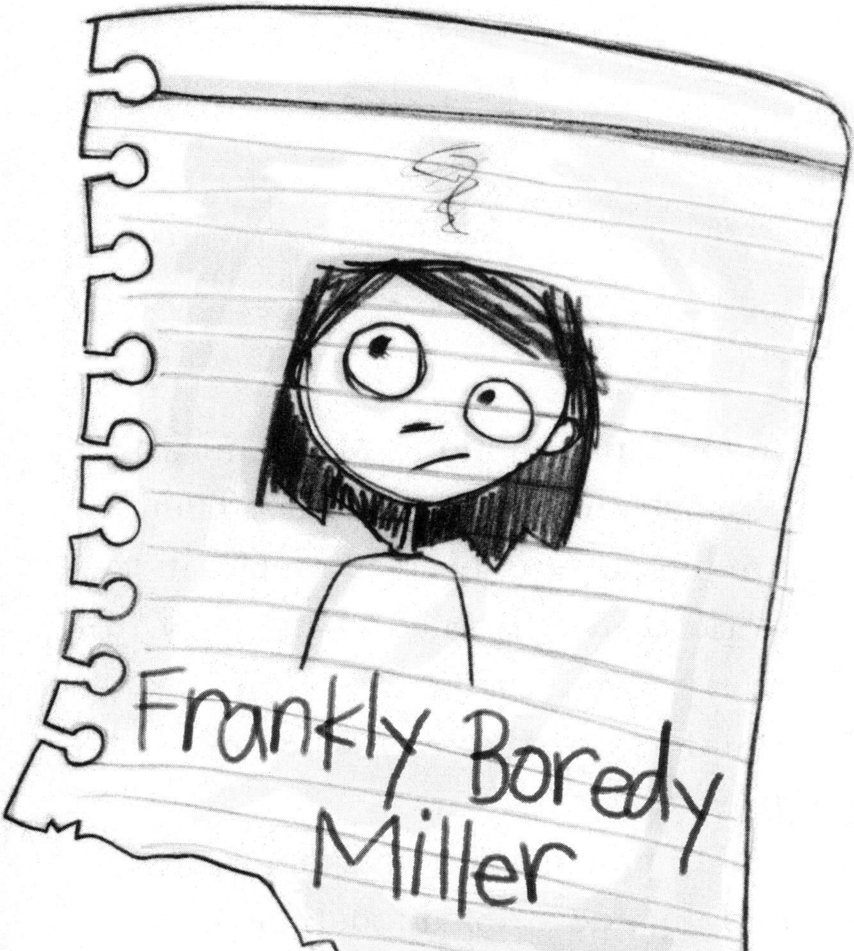
Frankly Boredy
Miller

CHAPTER 5

On Monday night, Mr. and Mrs. Wilson came over for dinner. They are my parents' bestest friends in the world. I like them because they talk to me like I am a real-life person, which is not the way all grown-ups talk to kids.

My mom let me wear her apron and my dad stapled together scrap paper so I could be the waitress and write down everyone's order on a pad. I went around the table, one by one, just like my favorite waitress, Betsy, does at Longfellows.

"May I take your order?" I asked Mr. Wilson.

"I will have the prime rib, rare, a pound of potatoes, a gravy boat, and yam soup."

"That will be one chicken pot pie and salad coming right up," which was **actually** what we were having for dinner.

"May I take your order?" I asked Mrs. Wilson.

"I will have thirteen slices of pizza, a frog leg sandwich in razzle-dazzle sauce, and asparagus lemonade."

"One chicken pot pie and salad coming right up."

Then I sat down and watched my

mom bring out the food that was too hot and too heavy for me to carry.

When we were finished with dinner, my dad let me be the busgirl. I'm a very good table clearer. Everyone thinks so and **that is not an opinion**.

Over dessert, they talked about who our mayor would be. Even though politics are boring, I felt very grown-up when they asked if I would vote for Frank Meloy.

"Does Frank Meloy carry a briefcase?" I asked.

"I think he does, yes," my dad answered.

"Then he's the person I would vote for," I announced.

"Because of the briefcase?" Mrs. Wilson asked.

"Not only. Also because both our names start with the same four letters. *And* because he carries a briefcase."

"Plus, he has a very good résumé," my mom said.

I looked up. "Résumé?"

"That's a list of all the jobs and schools a person has worked at and attended. You need one to get a job," said my mom.

"What's one look like?" I asked.

"I have some in my briefcase, actually," my dad said. "People applying to work at my office have sent me their résumés to look over. If you get me my briefcase, I'll show you one."

Before he even finished the sentence, I had his briefcase on his lap. He popped it open, pulled out

a small pile of papers, and handed
me the one on top. I held it very
carefully. I knew it was paper, but
still, it was very professional paper
and I did not want to make a crease.
Then I got a great idea.

"Can I borrow this?" I asked.

"If you're very careful," my dad said.

I looked right into his eyes.
"I will be very
careful."

"Then my
answer is yes."

After dinner I sat at my desk and pulled out my nicest paper. **If I brought my résumé with me to the radio station visit, then certainly I could get a job.** And if I brought business cards like the ones my dad has, they might want to give me a job even more. Business cards are for leaving your phone number and e-mail address with other business people. If you have a card, then nobody has to go looking for a pen and paper. My dad once showed me how he brings them to meetings and leaves them on a table all spread out like a fan.

I found a very serious pen that did not have an eraser and I looked at the résumé from my dad in order to write mine. I carefully put down all of my jobs—**Table Clearer, Temperature Taker, Mustard Sniffer**. When I was done, I put it in my dad's old briefcase, which I found in the basement, along with some other workerish things like paper clips, a legal pad, an old cell phone, and an old pair of glasses with the lenses missing. And when I finished that, I cut up an empty Kleenex box and made business cards that said:

Mrs. Frankly B. Miller
Radio Show Host
914-555-1819
MrsFranklyB@Millers.com

I put those in my briefcase as well. I was so excited, I almost couldn't fall asleep that night. I knew that if they liked my résumé and business card at the radio station, there was a chance they'd give me a job!

CHAPTER 6

Even though Millicent was also
my special buddy for the bus, the
ride to the radio station was still fun.
Everyone was so **excitified** that
we filled the air up with extra loud
chattiness. I could tell that Mrs. P. was
happy, too. **A for instance of what
I mean** is that she led us in a round
of my favorite clapping song!

Double, double this this

Double, double that that
Double this, double that
Double, double this that

Before my clapping hands even knew
it, we were at the most professional radio
station building I'd ever seen. On the
street we lined up with our special
buddies and then, when Mrs. Pellington
said we could, we **roundy rounded**
inside the building using a revolving door!
Inside, there were lots of people rushing
around importantly. Elliott's mouth
dropped off his entire face. He pointed.

"You. Are. Not. Going. To. Believe.
This." I followed his finger. There was a
little store with at least a **hundredteen**
shelves of candy and gum! I had, had,
had to work there. I never knew that
work buildings had places to buy candy.

For breakfast! Even Millicent looked up from her book to see all the deliciousity. And Elizabeth seemed really excited, too. Her smile wasn't nearly as big as mine or Elliott's, but I'm really smart about amounts of excitement, so I knew she was happy. But then, you will not even believe the rest. It is a scientific fact that:

1. There were turnstiles **INSIDE** the building
2. We had to get our picture taken
3. The picture was put on a special, real-life professional pass
4. That
5. We
6. Got
7. To
8. KEEP!

I almost hyperventilated from the excitement of it all. I held on really tightly to the pass even though it was fastened to a necklace made of tiny, little silver balls. I kept looking at the pass and every time I saw my face on it, my heart started thumping extra hard.

Then we got in a line, and a very nice lady handed out white stickers for name tags. We took turns waiting for the magic marker, which gave me time to think. When it was my turn, I very carefully wrote my name in the **neatest** letters my hand could make: MRS. FRANKLY B. MILLER. When it was Millicent's turn, Elliott tapped her on the shoulder to get her to stop reading. His tap said, "I wish *I* was Frannie's buddy."

Then we went through the turnstiles in the lobby to a bank of elevators. There were eight elevators there. Just like in the Chester Mall! When I looked over at Elliott, he sent me big-buggy eyes which meant he was also hyperventilating.

When we got into the elevator, Mrs. Pellington pressed sixteen. And that's when I knew just how lucky a day this would be. My **very luckiest** number in the universe is seven, and one plus six equals seven. When the doors opened, we could hear *The Sandy Sanders Show* over the loudspeaker. There were a **machillion** framed posters on the wall, and one of them read: THE SANDY SANDERS SHOW. I imagined another poster right next to it that read: THE FRANKLY B. MILLER SHOW.

When Mrs. Pellington told us to hold hands with our buddy, Elliott looked back at me with sad eyes. Millicent took my hand, but I could tell she wished it were a book.

A lady who sat behind a big, round desk pointed us to a waiting room with lots of radio magazines. There was a bowl of mints on the table, which Mrs. Pellington quickly took away. That's when I pulled out three business cards from my briefcase and fanned them out right where the candy had been. Elliott looked very impressed. So did other kids in my class. Drew asked me if he could have one. But he didn't have a job to give me, so I had to say no.

THE FRANKLY B. MILLER
SHOW

EVERY DAY AT 4 PM!

When Mrs. P. came back, she gave the longest, most **boringest** speech in the entire universe. And the worst part was that she looked at me the whole time!

As she talked, I realized that I had to go to the bathroom. I wanted to hold it

in as long as possible because that felt like something an adult would do. But after a little while, I was not so sure how adults did this because it was getting very hard to sit still. **I jittered** my knees. **I crossed** my legs. **I stood** up.

I sat back down. I stood up again. Finally, Mrs. Pellington said, "Frannie, what on earth is going on with you?"

Now was my chance to tell her, but I was too embarrassed to say it in front of my whole class.

"My legs are very excited," I said.

"Well, sit back down, please. You can

stand when the tour guide gets here, which should be any minute."

I sat back down and realized right then that I was not adult in the holding in way. I needed to get Mrs. Pellington alone so I could tell her this in a whisper.

CHAPTER

The tour guide's hair was dyed purple but just at her bangs. I wondered if her parents were really mad about that. She was very bouncy. I think she was even more excited than we were. I guess Elizabeth already forgot the part about not being rude because before she could stop it, she blurted, "Where's my dad?"

"He's doing his show, silly! And when he's done at ten o'clock, he will show you all the inside of the actual radio studio. And you will each get the chance to sit in the host's chair."

That's where we all **ooohed** and **ahhhed**.

"Okay, class, let's get in line," Mrs. Pellington said. I took Millicent's hand with my left one and held my briefcase with my right. We followed the tour guide down the hallway. The tour guide's name was Tuesday. I had never heard a person named after a day of the week. This was very interesting to me, especially because Tuesday was not **actually** the best day of the week.

Off the long hallway were some of the twenty offices that Mr. Sanders had told us about. I tried to peek and see what radio offices looked like, but we were walking too fast. All I saw was a tray with a stack of paper in it. When I got home, I had to remember to put a tray with a stack of paper on my desk.

Finally we stood in front of a huge glass window and inside we saw Mr. Sanders wearing headphones and talking and laughing into a microphone.

There was a machine in front of him with a lot of buttons, and Mr. Sanders pressed some but not others. He looked really professional with headphones on. It was the most **gigantic** room ever. There was a big, black sign and in red neon it yelled, "ON AIR." When I got home I also had to remember to make an ON AIR sign for my bedroom.

The door to the studio was really thick and had a sign that read: DO NOT

OPEN THIS DOOR! There were so many things I needed to remember, but I was in pain because I **REALLY, REALLY** had to go to the bathroom.

"We'll come back when the show is over and then we'll go inside and Mr. Sanders will give everyone a chance in front of the microphone," Tuesday said. "Now, I want to give you a tour of the offices."

How would I pay attention to all the offices if the only thing I could think about was how badly I had to go to the bathroom?

Everyone started to follow Tuesday down the hall, and I raised my arm and Mrs. Pellington called on me. I waved my hand at her so she'd come over to me and I could whisper.

When she bent down, I said very

quietly, "I *really* have to go to the bathroom." She gave me a bothered look, but then called Tuesday over, who said the bathroom was just right down the hall.

Millicent and I ran down the hall with my briefcase slapping against my leg, and when I opened the bathroom door, Millicent banged into it. Do you want to know why? Because she was reading! While she was running!

"Millicent!" I scolded. "You are not paying attention!"

"I am *too* paying attention!" she said. "But in the book, Jackie just told Joanna a secret, but Joanna got the secret wrong!" Secrets interested me. Maybe Millicent could tell me the secret later when we weren't rushing.

The bathroom was the biggest I'd ever seen. It was as big as the radio studio! There was an **actual** real chair, like the kind we had at home in our living room! And there was a basket of makeup that was free! And another basket with candy! This made Millicent put down her book. Elliott was not going to believe this.

I went to the bathroom as fast as is **scientifically possible,** and then Millicent and **I** went to catch up with our class. But when we came out of the bathroom, our class wasn't standing where it stood before. We didn't see anyone anywhere. I looked at Millicent, who looked just as confused as I was.

"What should we do?" she asked.

"I don't know!"

She grabbed my hand, and we ran down the hall. As we neared the studio door, I noticed that it was open and no one was inside hosting the show!

This was not a good sign and I knew it. I looked at the clock and it said 9:45 AM. That meant there were only fifteen minutes left of the show. Which meant it was the end of the show, which meant it was the call-in part of the show—the part where Mr. Sanders gave advice. Maybe my parents weren't the only ones who thought he wasn't good at this part of the show. Maybe someone told him and he got upset and left? What if he was crying by himself in his office? If that was the case, then who would do the advice part? I know that I give really good advice because

sometimes my dad says to me,
"Good advice, Bird!"

I felt sad Mr. Sanders was so upset
that he had to leave his own show, but
I also knew the saying "The show
must go on!" It couldn't go on without
Mr. Sanders, though. Unless . . .
Unless . . .

I looked at Millicent, who looked
stumpified.

"We have to go in there to help
Mr. Sanders," I said.

"We're not allowed!" she protested.

"But it's an emergency!" I cried.
Mr. Sanders was going to really
appreciate this. He'd probably give
me my own radio show.

I grabbed Millicent's hand and ran
inside the studio. She closed the door
behind us and looked really worried.

"We're going to get in trouble," she said.

I ran over to Mr. Sanders's chair and put my briefcase on the table. Then I clicked it wide open and took out the things that made me look **workerish**. I put the glasses with no lenses on my face, but they were too big and fell off. Then I sat in Mr. Sanders's chair (which was still warm) and put on his headphones. Those slid right off my head, too, but I adjusted them so they'd fit better.

When I looked over at Millicent, she had forgotten about getting in trouble because she was on the floor, reading the last pages of her book. Just then I heard a smacking sound. There was a man behind a glass window and he had headphones on, too! He was banging on the glass and pointing. **I gave a big smile because I knew he was trying to thank me for saving the day.**

Just then the phone rang, and I looked at Millicent.

"Should I answer it?"

Without looking up, she said, "Well, it is the advice part of the show."

She was right. It **was** the advice part of the show. I **had** to press the blinking light. I **had** to answer the phone. As I reached toward the blinking light, there was even more banging on the window. Now, a different man was making signals with his hands. He looked like an umpire in a baseball game. And since my dad watches baseball games, I know what the signals mean. When the umpire shakes his head no while moving a hand across his neck, it means, "You're out!" That was what the man was doing now. He was saying that

Mr. Sanders was "out." Which meant he was in big trouble. A different man was making the "safe" sign, which meant I was safe to answer the phone.

I pressed the red blinking button. Then some people in the booth slapped their palms against their foreheads. Another guy put his head down on the table. They were really impressed.

"Hello?"

I heard my *hello* fill the headphones. I was a radio host! I was saving the day! I was **ON AIR**! It was the best feeling in the entire universe. **And that is not an opinion.**

CHAPTER

Right when I answered the phone, I saw Mrs. Pellington and my entire class race down the hall to watch me. I felt so much **pride-itity** that they were running back to see me. They must not have wanted to miss a centimeter of my show!

When they reached the window outside the DJ booth, Mrs. Pellington slapped her hands against the window, too. She did it over and over like people stamp their feet at games when their team is winning. **I felt so proud of myself.**

"Hello?" I said again.

I turned to smile at my class just then. The first face I saw was Elliott's. He breathed on the glass window and with his finger wrote: "WOW!" **I was WOWING everyone, even Elliott!** And he is very hard to wow. Then Mrs. Pellington tried so hard to come into the studio to be part of the action, but she couldn't get the door open. She motioned to Millicent, who was reading. Millicent was going to get in BIG trouble now because she was reading and not paying attention!

A woman's voice said, "Hi. Is this *The Sandy Sanders Show*?"

"Yes," I answered proudly.

"But you're not Mr. Sanders."

"No, I'm Mrs. Frankly B. Miller. I'm taking over for Mr. Sanders. Do you have a question?"

"Ahhhh . . . okay. Well, Mrs. Miller, I do have a question and I'm hoping you can help me with it."

That was my chance to say the thing Mr. Sanders always said: "I'll give it my best shot."

I was really good at this!

"My husband and I are having a little disagreement. He says the polls at Chester Elementary are open until 8 PM tonight, but I think they close at 5 PM like the post office. Who's right?"

I could not believe my luck! Someone was asking me the most adult question I've ever been asked in my entire life! I wanted to memorize the feeling and tell it to my parents and their parents and their parents' parents and everyone's parents! I looked over at Mrs. Pellington, whom I imagined was thinking how much I'd grown up since the *Cambridge Magazine* visit. Mrs. Pellington was holding one hand to her chest and the other to her open mouth. **It** is a **scientific fact** that people do that when they are really happy that someone is saving the day.

It was a good thing that I was also good at doing two things at once. **I was very good at daydreaming and listening at the same time,** which is how I remembered that Mrs. Pellington said that thing about how the elections wouldn't be at our school anymore.

"Well, actually, you are both wrong," I said. I couldn't believe my own ears! **I was telling one adult that she and *another* adult were wrong and I wasn't even getting in trouble for it!**

"What do you mean?" the woman asked.

"The election moved. It's not even *at* Chester Elementary School. It's somewhere else."

"It's somewhere else? Well, where?"

I **squinched** my brain to try and remember where Mrs. P. said all the elections would be. And then, I remembered!

"The local theater!" I said.

"You mean the Morristown Playhouse?"

"Yes! The Morristown Playhouse. That's the local theater."

"But that's in Morristown!"

"Well, they don't have voting in schools anymore. It's a new rule. You can only vote in local theaters, so everyone has to go to the Morristown Playhouse if they want to vote."

The strangest thing is that when I

said these words, they didn't make a lot of sense, not even to my own two ears. But I was saying exactly the words Mrs. Pellington said, so they had to be true. Then an even stranger thing happened. I heard voices talking in my headphones, and they weren't my voices!

"Bob, call Victoria. Get her down here. Now!" said one man's voice.

"Little girl? Little girl? Can you hear me? Get off the mic. Get off the mic," said a woman's voice.

A different man said, "Steve, Victoria doesn't have the master key. Get Sandy, he's got a copy. Or get a janitor!"

I did not understand the code words of radio station people. But I would make sure to ask them what everything meant later. Now there were several people at the door, trying to get it open! People were trying all different keys. That's how much they wanted to come and watch me!

I looked over at Millicent with the biggest grin that my face ever invented. And that was the exact moment she reached the last page in her book and looked up. Mrs. P. motioned for her to open the door.

"It's locked," Millicent called, confused.

When I looked over at the door, I saw the janitors searching their gigantic key chains for the right key. Even they wanted to personally congratulate me. And then Mr. Sanders came back! Sometimes after being upset with my parents, I come downstairs to let them know I'm feeling better. I guess that's what Mr. Sanders was doing now. I wondered if it was a good time to give him my résumé.

Just then, I looked down and not just one line was blinking red for me, but **ALL THE LINES WERE BLINKING RED FOR ME**! I felt more important than a doctor!

As I went to answer another call, a high-pitched shriek came through the headphones. It was so loud that it hurt, and I had to throw the headphones off. When I put the headphones back on, there was no sound. I thought for at least one centimeter of a second that I was deaf. I tried talking into the microphone and was very relieved when I heard my own voice. What

I did not hear, though, was my own voice in the headphones like I did before. The microphone didn't make my voice sound louder than it was. That's when I got a very bad feeling.

I wished and hoped for one thing. And that was that I didn't break the radio station.

CHAPTER 9

At just the instant that I wondered whether I broke the radio station, the janitors opened the door, but the only person to rush in was Mr. Sanders. He ran toward me. I thought he was going to shake my hand or hug me or ask for my business card, but he didn't do any of those things. What he did, actually, was lift me up out of his seat and put me down right next to Millicent! Then he sat where

I was sitting and put the headphones back on his head. He started pushing buttons and pulling at levers. He didn't seem happy like I thought he'd be. I decided to wait and give him my résumé later.

Then Mrs. Pellington came rushing in saying, "I'm sorry, I'm sorry, I'm sorry!" What was she apologizing for? There was a lot more yelling back and forth. Mr. Sanders was yelling about circuits to the engineers, and the engineers were yelling about "kids today."

And then Tuesday, the tour guide, came rushing in with a very red face. She told us to hurry up and get out.

We were all so confused. We had only been there for forty-five minutes and we were supposed to be there for three entire hours! Drew started to complain that he didn't get to see as much as I saw. Then everyone (except Elliott, Elizabeth, and Millicent) complained that they didn't get to see anything, either! Mrs. Pellington was grabbing at her hands and looked more worried than I'd ever seen her. We didn't know why in the world we were leaving.

Going down the elevator wasn't as exciting as coming up. Passing all the important people and going through the turnstiles and saying good-bye to security wasn't as much fun. Instead, everything felt bad, like I had done something really wrong. Did I just have another *Cambridge Magazine* accident? No, it couldn't be that. I didn't spill anything on any originals. I didn't even see any originals to spill on. I was just trying to help Mr. Sanders.

We all stood crowded on the street, but our school bus wasn't there. "We're not supposed to be finished for another two hours!" said Mrs. Pellington, who sounded very worried. Then she started to dial her cell phone like crazy.

All my classmates surrounded me to ask a **machillion** questions about what it felt like to be on the radio. There was no way I could **actually** answer all of them. That's how many there were. I felt like a movie star. It was only when I realized their questions were getting hard to hear that I began to notice all the cars honking. The honking was really

bad, and when I looked up, I saw the
hugest traffic jam in the existence
of the planet. Drivers were getting
out of their cars and yelling at one
another. Other drivers were hanging
out of their windows waving their fists
in the air. I wondered if something
very bad had happened. I really
hoped not.

Mrs. Pellington was talking to the
people who worked in the lobby and
all they did was shrug at her. Even
when she said in her very worried
voice, "We're going to be stuck here
forever!"

But we weren't stuck there
forever. Even though it took a long
time, a bus finally came to pick us
up. There was so much traffic that
we didn't move a **centimeter** for a

really long time. In that really long time, Mrs. P. said she was too angry to speak, and that we would discuss this "𝐟𝐢𝐚𝐬𝐜𝐨" at our class meeting tomorrow.

CHAPTER

10

The second I walked into our house, my parents had their "You're in big trouble, young lady" faces on. I don't know how they already knew about the radio station visit.

I'd never seen my dad so **burning mad** before in all of my life. He had his arms crossed, and my mom had her hands on her hips. I didn't know what to do, so I just stood there, holding my briefcase, waiting for something to happen.

"You promised us you'd be on your best behavior!"

"I was!"

"Taking over a radio show was your best behavior?"

"It was an emergency! Mr. Sanders was in trouble!"

"It was *not* an emergency and Mr. Sanders was *not* in trouble!"

"He was, too, in trouble! He left the studio . . ."

"Mr. Sanders left the studio because he went to the bathroom!"

Huh?

The bathroom?

I hadn't even thought of that.

I had a very big trouble feeling.

"You were not thinking, Frances."

My mom **Frances-ed** me. I was in even bigger trouble than I thought.

"We are extremely upset with you," my father said as he began to pace.

"You caused absolute mayhem, not just for the radio station, but for the entire town!" my mother cried.

Huh? The entire town? **How in the whole wide world of America could that have been true?**

"There are still traffic jams out there," my father said.

I did not know what the traffic jams had to do with anything. Maybe my parents were so mad that they decided to blame everything bad that ever happened on me!

"Do you know how long it took me to get home?" my mother said, with her voice raised.

"How long?" I asked, but when she didn't answer I realized that it was a trick question. The kind you're not supposed to answer out loud.

"Where on earth did you get the idea that the polling station moved?"

This was an easy one!

"Mrs. Pellington told us that the election was canceled in all the schools!"

My father stopped pacing and faced me. He and my mother looked at each other confused. This news made them a little less angry, which meant I was not grounded for **foreverteen**—probably just forever.

"What did she say *exactly*?" my father wanted to know.

My father only asked for *exactly* things when he thought I didn't

have the facts straight. But **I DID**
have the facts straight.

"She exactly said something about
how there would be no more school
voting ever in the world. That it would
only be in local theaters," I said.

Now they looked even more
confused.

So I added, "Or something like that."

"But our town doesn't have a local
theater," my mom said.

"Oh yeah," I said. I forgot that
every time we wanted to see a play, we
had to drive all the way to Morristown.
Morristown wasn't local at all.

"So if our town doesn't have a local
theater, how could anyone in our
town vote there?" my dad asked me.

Now I was **stumpified**.

"I don't know."

I **squinched** my eyes close together to try and remember exactly what Mrs. Pellington had been talking about. And just then, I felt some little memories start to drizzle in.

A big ocean wave swelled inside my belly and up to my head as **I sort of, kind of, maybe, possibly, perhaps** remembered a tiny detail that must have fallen into one of my brain creases. Which meant there was a chance that I sort of, kind of, maybe, possibly, perhaps wasn't paying the most carefulest attention to Mrs. Pellington. **I was, however, (however is a very grown-up word)** paying the carefulest attention to note-passing with Elliott. And that's when I had the big realization and looked up at my parents with the guilt of the world in my eyes.

When Elliott and I started to pay attention, I thought Mrs. Pellington was talking about voting being moved from *our* school to the local theater, but she wasn't. She was probably still telling us the story she had started about her childhood. But, because I wasn't paying attention so well, I thought that by the time I started to pay attention she must have started a new story. I was in a worldwide canyon of trouble.

"Do you know what kind of trouble you created for everyone?"

See what I mean? I shook my head no. That was the truth of the world. I really didn't know. Now my father started pacing again.

"Well, first of all you gave out wrong information. The voting *was* at

Chester Elementary. That's why you were on a field trip all morning. To get you out of the way for the early morning voting rush. Second of all, you had no business sitting at Mr. Sanders's desk. Third of all, you had no right to answer a phone that wasn't ringing in your own home.

"There was a huge traffic jam today because all the Chester people and all the Morristown people were heading toward the Morristown polling place. By the time the Chester people finally figured out that they were supposed to vote at your school, they almost missed their chance to vote in the proper district! You might have cost Mr. Meloy the opportunity to be mayor. And he's the one you like!"

"Oh," was all I could manage to

say. The traffic jam was my fault? I felt terrible. I hadn't meant to do anything wrong at all. In fact, I meant to do the exact opposite of wrong.

"I was just trying to be an adult."

"Do you know what you're doing when you pass on information before getting the facts straight?" my mom asked.

I shook my head no. Again.

"You're starting rumors," she answered.

"Oh."

"That's a pretty kiddish thing to do, huh?"

Finally, a yes I could shake my head to.

Then my dad had a very good idea. "Let's go make dinner and we'll discuss this some more later."

I followed them into the kitchen, where they turned on the news, and guess what the top story of the day was? *Mrs. Frankly B. Miller nearly ruins it for the community.* It felt terrible. I had a very heavy weight on my shoulders.

That was definitely not the way I imagined hearing about myself on the radio!

CHAPTER 11

My parents didn't seem to want
my help in the kitchen, so I sat in the
dining room and stared at my dad's
old briefcase. I felt sad that my résumé
was still in there. It didn't even get
the chance to see any of the exciting
offices at the radio station. Come
to think of it, neither did I. Come to
think of it again, neither did anyone
in my class. **I was starting to realize
that saving the day might have actually**

ruined it. **What in the world was a person in my position supposed to do?**

Then I heard this on the radio: "*It's still unclear which way the election will go. It was a straight shot for Frank Meloy before Mrs. Frankly B. Miller steered our entire town in the wrong direction.*"

I slumped down in my chair.

For the first half of dinner, I thought maybe a miracle had occurred and my parents forgot all about the big mess of today's events. They were laughing and talking about their day and something funny that my father's assistant did. But at the part about family news, my parents put their serious faces back on.

"Do you remember that conversation we had about emergencies?" my dad asked.

I squinched my face to try and remember. Then I pressed my hands against my head so my memory would work and *Va-Voom!*

"Yes," I said.

"What's an emergency?"

"When there is a big accident or catastrophe. Something you tell an adult."

"Looking back, do you really think, in your heart of hearts, that there was an emergency in the radio station?"

I did not like where this was going. "No."

"And looking back," my mother added, "do you see how your actions affected the radio station and the entire community?"

"Yes," I said, and a tear ran down

my face. My parents did not like when I cried, but even though they leaned closer and my mom even put her hand on my arm, they did not say anything comforting.

My dad fixed his face so it looked nice and professional at the same time. This was his speech face.

"I know that you want to be helpful. And we think that's a wonderful quality to have. But you need to know when you are helping and when you are creating more trouble," he said. I nodded, but he was not finished.

"I know that sometimes you think you know as much as adults."

I looked up at my dad. That sounded exactly right.

"But even adults follow the rules.

And you didn't follow the rules. When people tell you not to touch something, then everyone, adults included, respect that and they do not touch that something."

"Rules are there for a reason," my mom said. "And when you go against the rules you get yourself into trouble."

That was true, too. This was the second time in two months I got into trouble by breaking the same rule.

"For the next two nights, there will be no TV watching. Instead, we're going to let you use that time to think of a way to make things better," my dad said.

"And, no playdates with Elliott next week," my mom told me.

My eyes almost fell off my face. "Why?"

"So you'll have more time to think about what it means to break the rules," my dad said.

That night, when I was lying in bed trying to fix the entire world, more things leaked into my brain creases. When I was in the radio station and everyone was banging against the glass, they were not doing it to show excitement. They were trying to stop me. I thought they were being like umpires and telling me I was getting a home run and that Mr. Sanders was out. But they were just trying to tell me that I was

saying the wrong thing to the entire
planet of the world.

That's when I got out of bed and
clicked my dad's briefcase open. I
took out my résumé, and very
carefully put it in the garbage.

CHAPTER 12

The next morning, I woke up with the worst butterflies. I had to face my entire class AND Mrs. P. I still didn't know exactly how I would make things better. But when I saw the headline of the newspaper, I felt a machillion percent relieved.

FRANKLY, FRANK WON, ANYWAY!

This was a very good sign. I looked at the picture of our new mayor and, frankly, he looked very happy. Like he just remembered it was his birthday! Everything was all fixed! What a big relief.

When I sat down for breakfast, the first thing my dad asked me was, "Do you have any ideas for how you're going to make things better?"

"But Frank Meloy won!" I said. "Everything is all fixed."

"Frank Meloy's winning doesn't erase the fact that you broke the rules."

"It doesn't?" That didn't seem fair. They just looked at me like I should know the answer.

My mother drove me to school in silence. I trudged up the stairs to my classroom feeling like I was about to take a thousandteen tests at one time.

Mrs. P. gave two long claps followed

by three short ones and we all sat down and paid attention. Elliott passed me a note.

Are you in trouble? it asked.

"Class, we need to have a very serious discussion about yesterday's antics."

Yes, I wrote back.

"We are all going to compose a letter to Mr. Sanders to apologize for what happened yesterday."

"I think Frannie should be the one to write it," Elizabeth said.

I frowned. Note-writing was one thing, but writing long letters was hard and also boring.

"We are all going to write it, but Frannie is going to come to the front of the class and lead us through it. Frannie, will you come here, please?"

I walked to the front of the class. I did not like being the center of attention when I was not saving the day.

"We want to tell Mr. Sanders the lessons we learned from yesterday. Can you tell me what those lessons are?" Mrs. P. asked. This was not a trick question.

"To keep your hands to yourself?" I answered.

"Good," Mrs. Pellington said as she wrote the answer on the board. "What else?"

"To pay attention?"

"Very good. What else?"

"Don't wander off or take matters into your own hands?"

"Excellent."

I beamed, very proud that she said

"excellent." That's when I started
to understand how to make things
better. I had to show that I knew
that what I did was wrong. I was
going to ask Mrs. P. if I could deliver
this letter to Mr. Sanders myself.

CHAPTER 13

The very next morning was
Saturday. At breakfast, I told my
parents what I wanted to do. Before
I knew it, my mom was on the
telephone making a **thousandteen**
calls and before I knew it again, we
were in the family car driving to the
new mayor's house. There were a lot
of photographers waiting on his lawn,
and when my mom and I walked up the
path, they looked at us but didn't take

any pictures. My mother rang the bell
and I started to get butterflies, and
this time I also felt moths! I had to
remember to tell Elliott about this fact.

A woman opened the door.

"Can I help you?" she asked us.

"Yes, I called this morning.
Mrs. Frankly B. Miller would like to
apologize to Mr. Meloy," my mother said
to the lady. Then the lady smiled at my
mom and looked at me with a wink.

"Certainly," she said. "I'll be right
back." Then she shut the door and
I looked at my mom and we waited
and waited.

Finally, the door opened, and there
was the actual future mayor of Chester
himself. I heard the flashes of the
photographers in the background. The
mayor held up his hand to them and

they stopped! His hand was like a magic wand! Then he reached out his other hand to my mother and with the smallest smirk (**I'm really smart about small smirks**) said, "Mrs. Frankly B. Miller. I didn't think I'd ever have the pleasure."

My mom shook his hand and said, "Mr. Meloy, congratulations. My name is Anna Miller. This here," she pointed to me, "is Mrs. Frankly B. Miller." And that's when the mayor's small smirk turned into a **very big, beaming smile**.

"Well, I'll be." Then he looked at my mother and winked. "You're very young-looking to be a Mrs.," he said.

"I'm not *really* a Mrs.," I said, because I wasn't sure if he was joking. "I'm just a kid."

"Indeed, you are."

Then my mom nudged me and said,

"Don't you have something to say to Mr. Meloy, Frankly?"

"Yes. Mr. Meloy, I wanted to say that I am a millionteen sorry for any trouble I caused you. It's my whole entire fault. I'm really sorry that I almost ruined your big election."

"Well, I appreciate your apology and I accept it. Would you care to have your picture taken with me for the newspaper?"

"Yes, very, very, very much," I said. Then he took my hand, and I followed him onto his front lawn.

"Ladies and gentlemen," he said to the photographers, "I'd like you to meet Mrs. Frankly B. Miller!" That's when all the photographers burst into little laughs and some people even clapped. Then there were lots and lots of flashes. The almost-mayor of Chester stooped down, put his arm around my shoulder, and smiled for a **machillion** pictures. At the very end of the pictures, I turned to him and asked him the most important question of the world.

"Mr. Meloy?"

"Yes, Frankly?"

"Can I send you my résumé?"

He laughed and patted me on the head.

"Frankly, I'd like nothing more," he said. It was the best day of my entire worldwide life.

When we got back in the car, I looked at my mom and she asked, "Ready?"

"Ready," I said. Time for stop number two.

Mr. Sanders opened his own door and seemed happier to see me than I ever would have imagined. I gave him the letter from my class and

apologized to him. And guess what!
He **also** accepted my apology!
Then he invited us inside his house for
some tea and cookies.

His house didn't have any assistants
or radio stations. And even though
it only had one office, it was still very
nice.

My mom and I sat at the kitchen
table with Mr. Sanders. He told me
that yesterday he was very upset
by what I did, but that when he
thought about it more, he realized
I was a very special kid. He said he
was very impressed that I wanted
a job. Then he told me that I
reminded him of his own self at my
age. I wasn't sure this was good
because I'm a girl and he's a boy,
but my mom told me later it was

a compliment. **I'm not so smart about compliments.**

Then Elizabeth came downstairs, and we all talked and laughed. We decided that Tuesday was a very good name and that when I was eighteen, maybe I could have Tuesday's job! This was the most excited I'd been since I got my picture taken just a little while ago.

CHAPTER

When I opened my bedroom door the next morning, there was a newspaper on the other side waiting for me. On the very front page of the *Chester Times* was a picture of me hugging the mayor! I picked it up and ran downstairs. I could barely believe my own eyes. A HAPPY ENDING FOR FRANK & FRANKLY was the headline! I would **never ever** throw this newspaper away.

I spent that entire Sunday smiling.

I didn't think I could ever get any happier.

But I was wrong.

That night, my dad and mom came into my bedroom. My dad had something behind his back, but I couldn't see it.

"We're very proud of you," my dad said.

"Apologizing is hard to do, and you handled it just like a pro," said my mom.

"Thank you," I said.

"We thought you might like this," my dad said as he pulled out a present from behind his back and gave it to me. I opened it excitedly. And when I looked at it, I gasped the biggest gulp of air imaginable. It was a picture frame, and inside the frame was the picture of me and the mayor from the newspaper. I put it on the nightstand next to my bed where I could look at it forever.

"We're very proud of you," my mom said, as she turned out my lights and closed my bedroom door almost all the way shut but not entirely. I lay in bed filled with so much pride-itity that I had done something that was actually grown-up.

Even though I still felt grumpy about not having a playdate with Elliott for one entire week, I felt like a real grown-up. I did all the right things. I knew I did, too, because I was going to sleep with no moths or butterflies.

But before I fell asleep, I remembered the most important thing. I got out of bed and walked over to my garbage

can. My résumé was lying at the
bottom, and I pulled it out and put it
next to my bed. Tomorrow morning,
my mom said she'd take me to the
post office. I was going to put
my résumé in a professional
envelope and send it to the mayor.
He probably needed someone like me
in his office.

THE END.

For my aunt, Maggie Stern, maker
of real-life sock dolls, and all the Sterns
and Stuarts in NYC and beyond!—AJS

Thanks as always to everyone at Penguin: Francesco
Sedita, Bonnie Bader, Caroline Sun, Christine Duplessis,
Jordan Hamessley, Meagan Bennett, and my editor,
Judy Goldschmidt. To Julie Barer, of course, and her
assistant, William Boggess. To my friends and family
for their support, and to Lili Stern for telling me that all
kids want to be veterinarians.—AJS

FRANKLY, FRANNIE

Doggy Day Care

by AJ Stern • illustrated by Doreen Mulryan Marts

CHAPTER

It is a **scientific fact** that I had three **fantastical** ideas in one day. It all started the morning I returned Herbert, our class rabbit. Everyone gets a chance to take him home for one entire night. When it was my turn, our teacher, Mrs. Pellington, said, "Frannie, do *not* do anything with Herbert other than feed him, watch him, and clean his cage."

I looked Mrs. Pellington right

in the eyeballs and promised her I would not do *any* of her **Do Nots**. It is a good thing she said something because I was going to practice a new haircutting style on Herbert.

I'm so good at cutting hair; I am considering being a professional haircutter. The only thing is, I don't think they have offices, and if you don't already know this about me, I love offices.

When I returned Herbert the
next day without any haircuts or
even **seventeen-one-hundred**
teeny tiny ponytails all over him
(which is **a for instance** of a new
style I'm working on) Mrs. P. was
so **impresstified** that she said in
front of my entire class, "Frannie,
I'm extremely proud of you. You

are clearly very good with animals."
Clearly and *extremely* are very
grown-up words. I try and use adult
words as oftenly as possible.

My best friend, Elliott, was clearly
extremely happy for me because when
I looked over at him, he gave me a
double thumbs-up. My smile was so
big, it almost wrapped around my
entire head. And that is when I had
my first **fantastical** idea.

My dad always says people
should put their talents to good
use. Certainly, I hadn't realized I was
so talented with animals, but once I
found out I was, I planned to put it to
good use. So I decided to un-become a
haircutter and become a veterinarian,
instead. Although I'd never been to
a veterinarian before, I knew for an

actual fact that they had offices. I
knew because my parents **actually**
know a veterinarian. Dr. Katz. In my
head, I spell it *Dr. Cats*, but it is a
scientific fact that he spells it
with a K. And a Z.

And if you didn't know this about
me, you should probably also know
that last week, I had planned on
being our mayor's assistant. But he
actually never called me after I sent
him my résumé. (A résumé is a list of
all the offices you've worked at.) So
my parents said I should think about
other jobs.

During recess, I told Elliott that
I was changing jobs. He asked me if

he could be a doctor with me at my veterinarian's office. I told him no, because I really needed a secretary.

Then his eyes nearly flew out of his head, across the room, down the stairs, and out the door. "I have *always* wanted to be a veterinarian secretary!" he said, even though I knew that was not a scientific fact.

Last week, Elliott wanted to be the assistant to the assistant (me!) of the mayor and yesterday he wanted to be an assistant to a haircutter (also me)! That is because (and I am not saying this in a bragging type of way) Elliott likes to copy a lot of things I do. Wanting to have a job is just one of those things he copies. It's okay with me because my father says Elliott's copying is a compliment.

And also because he only wants to be an assistant.

"We can practice when you come visit me!" I said. Elliott was staying at my house this weekend because his parents were going out of town.

The timing couldn't have been more **extremely** or **clearly** perfect.

CHAPTER

When I got home, I was bursting out of my own skin to tell everyone my good news. That's why instead of yelling out "I'm home!" I yelled, "I'm a veterinarian!"

I ran up the stairs, down the hall, and into my room. I had an **incredible, extremely** plan. I was going to open my own veterinarian's office in my bedroom. If I wanted it to be ready in time for Elliott's visit on Friday, which was the day after tomorrow, I needed to get busy. Since I had never been to a veterinarian's office before, I had to take some good guesses at what one would be like.

I took all my stuffed animals off my bed and put them next to each other on the floor. They were now officially sitting in the waiting room.

I didn't know if veterinarians wore stethoscopes, but I was going to be the type of veterinarian who did. I opened my sock drawer and pulled out a pair of tights. I put them around my neck with one leg draping down each side. I tied the feet together to look like the round part at the bottom of the stethoscope.

I pushed my desk to the center of the room because that was the examining table. Then I moved one chair next to it. That's where I would sit and take doctor notes on all the animals' complaints. Okay, maybe the **actual** animals wouldn't complain, but their owners would! I put another chair on the far side of the room where Elliott would sit as my secretary.

I pulled out some paper and drew a lot of dog bones on them, then cut them up very carefully, putting each bone picture in front of all the waiting dogs so they didn't get hungry.

I was only going to be a dog veterinarian. Cats are too slippy. Every time I try to hug one, they always spill out of my arms. That is why I was only going to have dog patients.

I sat down and looked around. What was missing? **A doctor's coat!**

I heard my parents talking in the kitchen so I knew the coast was clear. Then I ran down the hall and into their bedroom, where I took a white, button-down shirt off of one of my dad's hangers. That would be my doctor's coat. I put it on, and with the tights hanging around my neck, I looked **actually** and **clearly** like the most professional dog veterinarian anyone has ever seen!

Back in my room, I made the official sign for the office:

Dr. Frannie B. Miller,
Profeshinal Vetiranerien

Dogs Only!

(Elliott Stephenson is the Secretary.)

I practiced listening to the dogs' hearts. But after a while, it was boring.

I needed to practice on real animals. In a real veterinarian's office. And the only way to do that was to **actually** work for a real veterinarian.

And that is when I had my second **fantastical** idea. I was going to retire from school and work for Dr. Katz! I *already* had a résumé. I just had to think of the perfect way to get my parents to agree.

CHAPTER

That night at dinner, I told my parents I had a lot of news. I was going to tell them in size order. Smallest news first, biggest news last.

"I have opened a dog veterinarian's office on the second floor. It's for live dogs, not stuffed ones. That is really a problem because I don't have any live dogs," I told them during the salad part of dinner.

This was the part where they were

supposed to get their own fantastical idea. My mom was supposed to say, "Well, maybe you could take some time off from school and work for Dr. Katz. What do you think, Dan?"

And my dad was supposed to answer, "I was just going to say the same thing!"

But my dad just said, "That *is* a problem!"

"We only have stuffed animals in this house," I continued. My parents looked at me with twisty smiles at their mouth corners.

"Those are good observations, Frannie," my dad said.

"I wonder if there is a kind of place that is not a zoo where there are a lot of animals. That would be a good place for me to go work at being a dog veterinarian since I actually and clearly can't do it here. You really need live dogs if you're going to practice being a dog veterinarian. You can't do that at the zoo because there aren't any dogs at the zoo. I wonder where you can do that. Do you happen to know?" I asked both my parents.

This was the part where they were supposed to suggest that I give up school and work for Dr. Katz. But they didn't do that here, either! All they did was this:

"A place that's not a zoo," my dad said, scrunching his eyebrows together. "I'll have to think on that."

"It would have to be a place where there were doctors and animals. A place where the doctors were the doctors *for* the animals, but again—

not a zoo. That is the exact type of place I need to work at. But, if I worked at a place like that, I probably wouldn't have much time for school."

"Okay, Frannie. Like I said, we'll think on it." Then my dad turned to my mom and said, "Did you hear that Bill and Janice are going to Italy for two weeks?"

"I did!" my mom said. "Rome . . . It's so exciting!"

Oh no! What was happening? The conversation was changing. If they didn't think I was serious about working for Dr. Katz, they'd never let me do it! The only way to prove my **seriousity** was to show them how much I know about dogs.

"Did you know that dogs come in all different sizes?" I interrupted.

"Even in Rome," I added so they didn't think I was too **interruptish**.

"I did," my dad said, helping himself to some spaghetti. "Just like people," he added.

"Some dogs are so little, you can carry them around in your pocket and you don't even have to walk them!"

"Is that so?" my mom asked, taking a sip of her seltzer water. It is a **scientific fact** that seltzer is a grown-up version of water.

"It *is* so. Did you also know that there are one thousand million different types of dogs? Someone at my school has a dog that is half poodle and half a different kind of dog and it is called a *Labradoodle*."

"A Labradoodle! What a funny name!" my mom said.

"Like I said, there are one thousand million different types of dogs. Labradoodle is just one of them. I certainly know a lot more types."

"I didn't know you were quite so informed about dogs, Frannie!" my mom said, **impresstified**. This was working!

"I am. I'm quite informed. Mrs. Pellington said I'm very good with animals. A natural." I added the part about being a natural. "My favorite types of dogs are Goldendoodles and Sheep Poodles."

I didn't actually know if these were real types of dogs, but when you're as good and natural with animals as I am, you're **probably usually** right.

"I also really like Skeedaddles and Puffdoodles."

"Wow, I've never heard of those types of dogs. Are you sure you're not making these up?" my dad asked with a small twinkle in his eye that said, *even if you are making these up, you seem so responsible and smart about dogs, if you happen to ask us if you can quit school to get a job as a veterinarian's assistant, we will say yes.*

I told them a little about Schnoodles and Bageegles, but when my mom turned to my dad to say something else about Rome, I stood up.

Sometimes you need to stand up to make announcements.

"I am sorry to interrupt, but I have something to tell you and it's very, extremely . . . official." My parents looked at me with their waiting faces. I was quiet for a minute and that's when I realized I'd need to use my English accent. English accents are very professional.

"Ahyve desoyded to ree-tiyah from school becawzz I am gowing to woohk for Dawktah Kaaatz," I announced in my absolute, **extremely professional** English accent.

I waited for them to respond, but

they didn't say anything. They just sat there with very confused expressions. That's when I realized they didn't understand my English accent because it was *too* amazing! They probably needed me to repeat it without the accent.

"I have decided to retire from school because I am going to work for Dr. Katz," I said in my regular voice.

But instead of saying "Let me call school right now and cancel!" or "That is the best and most professional idea we've ever heard!" my dad just covered my hand with his and said, "Frannie, you are a true original."

"You sure are, Frannie," my mom agreed. I learned the hard way that original means one-of-a-kind. One-of-a-kind is good if you are a person, but bad if you are wet paper. Especially when the original paper has **extremely professional** office words on it. And gets ruined because someone spilled something on it. Which is **a for instance** of something I did by accident when I was a kid one month ago.

These were not the reactions I wanted. When I opened my mouth to say more, the phone rang.

My mom hates it when people call during dinner, but **I love when people call, no matter when.** That's because when I answer the phone, my parents let me say, "Miller residence, this is Frannie. How may I direct your call?" Because that's how I've heard office people answer. But I was not allowed to pick up the phone during dinner.

The phone stopped ringing for a few seconds and then it rang again. Then it stopped and started again one more time, and my parents gave each other emergency looks.

When someone keeps calling, it usually means something is wrong!

CHAPTER

When the person called back a third time, my dad rushed out of his seat and picked up the phone. We could only hear his end of the conversation, and it went like this:

"Oh no! That's terrible. What happened? Uh-huh, uh-huh, you're kidding! Of course! Really? That's so exciting! Don't be silly. We'd be happy to do it. Oh, she'll love that!"

My mom and I looked at each

other. How can something be terrible and exciting at the same time?

"Okay, will do. We'll see you soon," my dad said.

When my dad sat back down, he looked upset.

"What is it, Dan?"

"Magoo broke her leg." Magoo is my dad's sister, which makes her my aunt. Her real name is Margot, but instead of saying that name when I was a baby, I said "Magoo." So it stuck.

"How?"

My dad looked right at me when he said the answer.

"She tripped over her dog!"

I could not believe my own eardrums! In **a million, trillion years** I would never trip over my dog. And that is **not an opinion.**

"So, what's the exciting part?" asked my mom.

This question really **excitified** my father. "A fancy New York toy store owner wants to look at Magoo's sock dolls. She's thinking of ordering a whole bunch of them!"

Magoo makes dolls out of socks. They are really cute and funny with buttons for eyes and yarn for hair. They are called sock dolls because they're made from socks stuffed with cotton. Some are plaid and polka-dotted. Some are striped. And others have lots of curly lines on them. I am really lucky because I have three. I can even make one myself. Magoo showed me how.

"But since she broke her leg she needs our help getting ready for the meeting."

That was when I remembered a **really important scientific fact**.

"But she's all the way in Massachusetts!" I told my father. "Which is really far from Chester."

"We'll have a road trip!" he said.

"But, Elliott!" I said before getting the terrible **disappointment drop** in my belly. "Will he be able to come with us?"

"He's more than welcome," my mom

said. That brought a big smile to my face, but I was sad we wouldn't get to use the practice veterinarian's office right away. "Let me call his parents and run it by them," she said, getting out of her seat.

"I left out the best for last," my dad said.

I looked up.

"Magoo has a job for you, and it has to do with her pets! I'll let her tell you herself, but it sure sounded like the perfect job for a budding veterinarian!"

I was so **excitified**, my brains almost fell into my spaghetti. I was going to show my parents that I was ready to work for Dr. Katz and quit school. I was going to show them by being really good with Bark,

Magoo's dog. Magoo also had three slippy cats—Hester, Esther, and Lester—but I'd let Elliott watch them because I was only a dog veterinarian. And that was my third **fantastical** idea in exactly one full day.

CHAPTER 5

It didn't feel like a long drive to Magoo's on Friday afternoon because as soon as Elliott and I got in the car, we fell asleep. What did take a long time was waiting for Magoo to answer the door!

We heard her yell, "I'm coming!"

But then we waited and the door still didn't open.

"Hang on! I'm almost there!" she called again.

Elliott and I looked at each other

and giggled. Adults are really weird sometimes. We heard lots of messing around with the doorknob, and finally Magoo opened the door.

Have you ever seen more than one really exciting thing at the exact same time and then you can't decide which thing to look at first? That is the exact same thing that happened to me!

Here is the blur of what happened. When Magoo opened the door, the first thing I saw was a cast that went all the way past her knee and up her thigh! But before I could even study it, Bark ran past Magoo, put his paws on my shoulders, and knocked me over. Elliott backed away really quickly because he got scared, and that is not an opinion.

Bark licked my face over and over with his pink, sloppy tongue. I squinched my eyes and mouth and turned my head away because **I do not** like being licked on the face. **I** really hoped getting your face licked was **not** part of being a veterinarian. I also hoped that Magoo and my parents didn't see me squinching. I needed them to think I was a natural with animals. Dogs especially!

"Bark must have really missed you," Magoo said.

My dad pulled me up, and I tried to wait until Bark turned his head before I wiped his licks off my face. I didn't want to hurt his feelings.

Besides the licking that I didn't like, there was so much about Bark I did like. **A for instance of what I**

mean is that Bark has the softest hair, and it feels just like fluff. He is white all over his body and has gray spots on the top parts of himself. He's very shaggy and always looks like he needs a haircut, but he doesn't. That's the way his hair is supposed to look. **I know that**

because once I tried to cut it off and Magoo caught me just in time to explain about shaggy dog hair.

"He's a Labradinger, right?" I asked Magoo. Now was my chance to show her how much I knew about dogs!

"No, just a plain old sheepdog," she said. She was certainly not right about that. I knew a **Labradinger** when I saw one. Then I remembered about introducing people.

"This is my best friend, Elliott."

Elliott and Magoo shook hands, and Magoo said, "Elliott, I don't know if you want a job as much as my niece does, but if you do, you're in luck."

"I do," Elliott said, excited, but then his face dropped a little. "But I already have a job. I'm Frannie's secretary."

My parents and Magoo laughed out loud, and Elliott and I looked at each other confused. Sometimes grown-ups don't know the difference between **funny** things and **not funny** things.

"Well, if Frannie will let you, I'd like to offer you the job of special assistant to cats."

Elliott looked at me and I looked at Magoo.

"Would he still get to be my secretary?" I asked Magoo.

"Absolutely," Magoo told me.

I looked back at Elliott and said, "Okay, you can take that job."

Then Magoo said, "Great, now come on in." She opened the door even wider. And that is when I saw that Magoo's cast was the most exciting one I had ever seen. It didn't have one single drawing or name on it like when kids got casts. It was perfectly clean and white and actually very **super extra professional-looking**. I couldn't take my eyes off it. But when Magoo took her crutches out from under her armpits and hopped to the side to get out of our way, I couldn't take my eyes off the crutches! They were the **most special** crutches I'd seen in the entire world of America. They were not wooden like the ones kids used; they were metal, which meant they were silver! Everyone knows that silver things are **very adult**.

Magoo's cast and crutches made her look very official. I wanted to reach my arm out toward them, but my dad saw inside my brain because just as I was reaching out for them, he said, "Don't even think about it."

I quickly pulled my arm away.

"How in the worldwide did you know what I was thinking?"

"I have special mind-reading dad powers," he said, even though I knew that was **not** actually a **scientific fact**.

We followed Magoo as she crutched her way around her house while we pointed out different things to Elliott. I had already been to Magoo's house so I felt very smart about everything that was there.

"What are those?" Elliott asked, pointing to the wall of shelves where her dolls lived.

"Those are my sock dolls," Magoo said.

"Oh yeah! Frannie has some in her room," said Elliott.

"Would you like to see one?" Magoo asked.

Elliott nodded his head up, down, up, down, like it was a horse on the merry-go-round. Magoo crutched over to the shelf.

"A boy one!" Elliott requested.

She brought back a boy sock doll, and Elliott studied it very closely, turning it around and around. He investigated the striped legs and polka-dot arms, the button eyes and the thick, brown nose stitches. He pulled gently on the thick, brown yarn that was cut short into boy hair. Then he looked up with an expression I'd never seen before.

"Are there any sock doll makers that are boys?" he asked Magoo.

"I believe there are, Elliott."

"Well, could I be a special assistant to cats, Frannie's secretary, *and* a boy sock doll maker?"

Magoo beamed. "I don't see why not!"

"Elliott!" I said.

"What?"

"I think that is too many jobs . . ."

"Why?" he asked.

"Because it is against the law to have so many."

"Oh," he said. I could not believe for the worldwide life of me that he didn't know that.

He thought for a minute.

"Maybe I can be a sock doll maker and special assistant to cats on weekends, and then your secretary during the week?"

I thought about this for one

point two moments and then I agreed to what sounded like a very good deal.

"I can't wait to show you how to make them!" Magoo told him.

Elliott handed the doll back to Magoo. "Thanks for showing it to me."

"You can hold on to it for now, if you want."

"I can?" Elliott could hardly believe his **worldwide** luck. I didn't feel badly because, like I said, I already owned three sock dolls.

We walked around Magoo's house a little more. There's always so much to investigate there because there are so many rooms. **A for instance of what I mean** is that she has a craft room, a sunroom, and a meditation room. That's a room for being quiet. Elliott and I were not so interested in that room. Plus, she has a gift closet, a television room, a playroom where the animals sleep, and then all the usual rooms.

I can tell my mom likes the quiet room the best because she popped her head in and said, "Oh, Magoo. It's marvelous what you've done with this space!"

Marvelous is a grown-up word, but it's not for me. It's very old-fashioned.

Elliott and I felt really lucky because we were going to sleep on couches in the sunroom. A sunroom is a room that is outside, like a porch, but has a screen on it, so that it is also inside. The sun gets to come into the room, and that is the **scientific fact** for how it got its name.

The cats meowed and rubbed up against my leg. I looked down, but I was not going to pick any of them up because I could tell just looking at them that they were the extra slippy kind of cat. I also wanted Magoo to see that I was a natural with dogs—not cats!

"What are the cats' names?" Elliott asked Magoo.

"Hester, Esther, and Lester," she said.

See what I mean about slippy? Slippy names for slippy cats.

CHAPTER 6

After settling in, we had a meeting. It was the most **boringest** meeting I'd ever been to. Elliott, too. I doodled in my head and passed notes to Elliott using just my brain waves. **I knew he was doing it, too, because we got boringified at the same things.** The only time it was not boring was when Magoo explained about the fancy toy store person.

"She's in town for only one day

and she is very interested in looking at my sock dolls because she might want to sell them in her store."

"It's just so exciting," my mom said. I could tell she really meant it because her eyes looked very sparkly.

"They have sock doll stores?" Elliott asked with his mouth wide open.

Magoo laughed. "It's more like a store that sells lots of toys and dolls. They've never sold this type of doll there before. But they're interested in looking at mine!"

Elliott and I looked at each other with WOW eyes.

"The point is," Magoo said, "this woman is coming to town especially to meet me. Since my leg is broken, she's offered to come here to see me instead of having me come to New York City with all my dolls. Now here's the very important part . . ." Elliott and I leaned in to make sure we didn't miss the very important part. "The toy store woman is very, very allergic to cats. Because I have three cats, we have to start cleaning very early on Sunday. We need to vacuum everywhere and close the cats up in the TV room. We have to make her visit as comfortable and itch-free as possible. There can't be cat hair anywhere."

"Do we get to come to the meeting?" I asked.

"Unfortunately, no," Magoo said. **Unfortunately** is a good grown-up word I needed to use more. "But, you *are* going to go in the car with your dad to pick her up on Sunday!"

"Fun!" I said. Elliott agreed.

"The most important thing is that there cannot be one single cat hair in this house."

Then my dad talked and told Elliott how to feed the cats. His instructions sounded like this: *Boring boring boring. Boring boring boring. A little more boring. Even **boringer.** One last time with the **boringest** of boring until finally, your ears close shut so you never have to hear anything boring again.*

"We all clear?" my dad asked. Everyone nodded yes. "Good, then let's get to work. This house needs to be in tip-top order for Magoo's big meeting, and Bark needs to be walked."

That was my cue. While Elliott went into the kitchen to open the smelly bag of cat food, I went and got Bark's leash from the front hall table. Then, I went over and clipped it to Bark's collar like a professional leasher!

That is when Magoo said, with a big *I forgot something* in her voice, "Oh, shoot—Frannie!" I looked up. "I forgot to tell you your job title."

I was so **excitified** to hear my title, I held my breath.

"I was so busy telling Elliott about his job, I forgot to tell you about yours. *You* are the president of cats."

Cats?

My mouth fell off my entire face.

"But, I am going to be a *DOG* veterinarian," I said. "Not a cat one."

"I know, sweetie," Magoo said. "But Bark is just too big for you."

"No, he's not too big. He's the perfect size," I said. And just when I said that, Bark jumped up on me and knocked me down.

"Sorry, sweetie. Maybe next year when you're bigger."

Next year? Next year I wasn't even going to want to be a dog veterinarian!

"Sorry, Bird," my dad said, taking the leash from me. Bird is my middle name. Please do not tell anyone. It is a **scientific fact** that my dad is the only one who calls me by it.

I looked over at Elliott in the kitchen. He was lining up three boring cat bowls. I looked back down at Bark. If I wasn't taking care of Bark, how would I prove that I was ready to be a dog veterinarian?

I dragged myself into the kitchen and helped Elliott pour the stinky food into the boring bowls. As my dad tugged on Bark's leash, Bark looked over at me and I could tell by his expression that he wished I

were the one taking care of him. His
eyes were very droopy, which meant
he was sad, and his breathing was
very fast and heavy, which meant he
was getting sadder by the second! I
looked over at my mom on the couch
to make sure she saw how sad Bark
was to leave me. But she was too
unfortunately busy picking a piece
of cat fur off her sweater to see the
tragedy.

When my dad and Bark left for
their walk, Elliott and I finished
feeding and watering the cats. Then
I **harrumphed** around and Magoo
taught Elliott how to make sock dolls.

That night before we got into
our couch beds, I did something to
show Magoo how thoughtful and
responsible I was. I hoped it would

make her change her mind and switch my job with my dad's job.

Sometimes when you go to Disney World and stay at their hotel, the housekeepers turn down your sheets and put a mint on your pillow. I decided I would do that for her, also. Except I couldn't find a mint. I looked all over the house for something sweet, but there wasn't anything. Finally, I grabbed a jar of strawberry jelly and put that on her pillow. Then I folded down her sheets.

Magoo would probably give me my dad's job caring for Bark the second she saw what I did!

CHAPTER

Elliott and I woke up on Saturday to the sun kissing us on our noses. We still couldn't believe our luck that we got to sleep inside *and* outside, almost. We shuffled into the kitchen just as my dad whistled for Bark to come take his walk. He came running with his big tail wagging.

Dad clipped the leash to his collar, and I couldn't believe that even with the turned down bed and strawberry jelly on Magoo's pillow, I still had to take care of the stinky cats. Dad said if Elliott and I wanted to come along, we should hurry up and feed the cats and put on our coats.

Outside, I memorized how he held the leash just in case his wrist stopped working and I needed to take his place. Then I memorized exactly the streets we walked down so that I wouldn't get lost when I finally got to take care of Bark myself.

"You are such a good Labradinger," I said to Bark. That is when Elliott pointed to the little dog rounding the corner running toward us. Then not even two seconds after, another person with their dog rounded the corner and then even more.

"What is going on over there?" my

dad asked. "It's like an animal parade."
Then a rabbit on a leash appeared. And
then a cat on a leash! We walked really
fast to the corner and, when we got there,
we saw even more people with their pets.

"Maybe it's an audition for animal
TV!" Elliott said.

"Anything's possible," my dad said.
We got closer. Finally when we got
close enough, I read the sign. You
will never in one million decades
guess what it said.

VETERINARIAN'S OFFICE!

My dad looked me right in the eyes
and that's how he knew exactly what I
was thinking.

"Don't even think about it, Bird."

"Just for one half of a centimeter of
a second?" I begged him.

"No. We have way too much to do. There are vets in Chester. You can wait until we get back home."

We weren't getting back home for another entire full day and a little! That was nearly **foreverteen** hours!

I dragged my feet and hung my head extra low on the walk back so my dad would know just how sad I was.

When we got back to Magoo's, Elliott and I saw her crutches leaning against the wall. We looked at each other. Maybe she was healed? Then two seconds later, Magoo rolled down the hall. She was in a wheelchair!

That is when I stopped breathing almost **forever**. I could not believe my **worldwide** eyes! Elliott was freeze-tagged into place.

For a second I thought Magoo

broke something else, but then she explained that she just needed to get off her foot for a while. Also the crutches made her armpits hurt. I knew that I would *never* get hurt armpits if I had crutches.

I thought walking on her silver crutches would be the most fun thing in the world. But when I saw the wheelchair, I changed it to the second most wonderful thing in the world.

Pushing Magoo in her wheelchair would be the most **extremely, honestly, number one-tastic, most official thing** that I ever did. If I showed Magoo how natural I was at pushing a wheelchair, she would know how good I was at taking care of people. And if I was good at taking care of people, then I'd probably be good at taking care of dogs. People are bigger than dogs.

"Do you need me to push you somewhere?" I asked her.

"No, I'm good where I am, sweetie. Thanks, though."

"Oh," I answered, disappointed. "Maybe you need me to walk on your crutches so they don't get stale?"

She laughed. "I think my crutches are okay."

"Because I know for a scientific fact that if you leave things out for too long they can go stale."

"Frannie," my dad warned.

"What?"

"You *know* what."

"I don't! I don't know what!" I argued.

"Aunt Magoo's wheelchair and

crutches are off-limits," my mom called from the couch where she was reading the newspaper.

Oh yeah, *that* what.

"Don't you worry about my crutches. I think they'll be just fine on their own."

That is not a fact I agreed with.

I walked over to the wheelchair and stood next to her. She was busy making a sock doll and wasn't paying so much attention to my *please can I wear your crutches* expression. Or even my *I'm probably the best wheelchair pusher-er in the world* face.

Elliott sat on the other side of Magoo, working on his own sock doll. They were being very concentrate-y and quiet. They were also being boring.

I put my hand on the handlebar part of the chair.

"Well, if you *did* need someone to push you, I bet I'd be really good at it," I told her.

Magoo looked up and smiled. "You know what? I would love it if you could push me into the kitchen so I could get a glass of water."

"OKAY!" I said. I was almost as excited as I was when I got to drive a bumper car. I got behind Magoo's chair and pushed it very slowly into the kitchen. It was much heavier than I thought it would be, but still, I was a very good wheelchair roller. I stood next to Magoo as she drank her water and then I pushed her back to the exact place she had been before.

"Do you need more water?" I asked.

"I just drank some, silly!"

"When you break something you get very thirsty," I told her.

"Really, is that a fact?" Magoo wanted to know.

"Oh," I responded, looking down. "Well, maybe not a *scientific* fact," I said.

"I'll let you know if I want more water."

"Okay, but if you need me to push you somewhere else really soon," I told her, "I could do that, too."

"Sounds like a deal," she said.

I waited. And waited. **And waited**. But Magoo didn't need to go anywhere. Then I got bored and decided to count how many rooms (including bathrooms and closets) Magoo had in her house.

When I went into Magoo's room, she yelled, "The boxes are off-limits!"

"Okay," I yelled back, even though I didn't know what she was talking about.

But then I saw them. There were three very big cardboard boxes, one next to the other. I went over to look.

One was filled with cloth and yarn, the next with buttons, and the next with socks and cotton! Because they were "off-limits," **I looked with my eyes and not with my hands,** as my dad would say.

Next to the boxes was a bag. Its mouth was wide open. I stood over it and looked inside, and you would not believe what was in it!

It was filled with a hospital amount of medical tape, Ace bandages, Band-Aids, and every single thing in the world that you could ever imagine or want. I didn't know which bag I liked more, my dad's briefcase or this one. I pulled it out and brought it with me into the living room to show everyone. It was not a box so it was okay that I looked with my hands.

"Look what I found!" I said.

Everyone looked at the bag.

"What is that?" my dad asked.

"It's supplies for my leg," Magoo explained.

"Frannie, where did you find that?" my dad asked in his *I'm a little bit annoyed with you* voice.

"It's not a box!" I argued.

"Frannie," continued my dad, "put that bag back immediately. You know you don't go through other people's personal belongings. You leave Magoo's things alone, okay? The Ace bandages, the medical tape, the crutches, the wheelchair, it's all off-limits. Do you understand? We need your help with the cats, not with the medical supplies."

"Fine," **I grumped**, and then dragged the bag back to Magoo's room, sat on her bed, and waited to become unbored.

CHAPTER

After we cleaned all the dishes
from dinner, we got to do whatever it
was we wanted until bedtime. Magoo
still had to work on her dolls because
tomorrow was the big day with the
fancy toy store person. Now she had
company, though. Elliott was working
so hard on his sock doll, it was almost
done! He was so good at it, I worried
he might not want to be my secretary,
after all.

"Frannie, would you like to start a new doll?" Magoo asked. "I can thread a needle if you need help."

"That's okay," I told her.

Making sock dolls is fun but I needed to concentrate on showing Magoo how responsible and thoughtful I am. Which is why I went looking again for something mintish to put on her pillow.

I still couldn't find anything so I took a big jar of honey and put *that* on her pillow. The jelly from the day before was on her night table, so I left it there.

Then I looked over and saw her crutches leaning up against her wall, looking very lonely. If Magoo wasn't going to use them, I didn't understand why I couldn't. They were just going to waste lying there against the wall like that. And also they were probably going stale.

I tiptoed down the hall and saw my mom and dad talking in the kitchen while they drank tea. Magoo and Elliott were busy with their dolls. This was the absolute perfect time! No one would even see me use the crutches so they would never even know that I used them, which meant I could never get in trouble!

I tiptoed back to Magoo's room and shut her door. As I walked toward the crutches, I heard a sound at the door. I opened it and there was Bark! He was always trying to tell everyone that he wanted me to be in charge of him instead of my dad. But no one understood this except for me because **no one really understood Bark the way I did**. I let him in the room and then I shut the door again.

The crutches were really tall. I wasn't sure how my armpits would reach the top. That was when I decided to drag the crutches over to the bed. Then I stood on the bed and set the crutches in a ready position. I leaned over and placed my armpits on the cushiony top part. Then, when both armpits were in their seats, I stepped off the bed. **But then something horrible happened**. My feet did not touch the floor, and I was swinging by my armpits from the crutches.

Bark came over to help me, but he knocked into the crutches, which slipped out from under me and I fell right on top of him. Bark yelped very loudly and leaped away, banging into the night table and knocking the picture frames and the jar of jelly to

the floor. The crutches crashed into the wall and then plunked down to the floor next to them, and I landed on my butt with a bang. There were **three million** different crashes, which is why the door flew open and I saw the **extremely worried** faces of my mom, dad, and Elliott.

"Are you okay?" my mother asked as she ran to help me up on my feet.

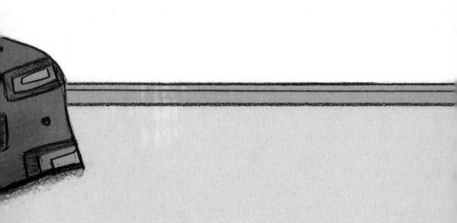

As soon as I told her I was fine, my dad's face filled with red, splotchy anger. Elliott put his hand over his mouth, and my mom put her hands on her waist, which is what she does when she is about to yell at me. **I was in a worldwide canyon of trouble.**

CHAPTER

After I fell off the crutches, my dad and mom had to think of an "appropriate" punishment for me. When they came back they told me that my punishment was that I could no longer go with my dad to pick up the **fancy** toy store woman.

"What about Elliott?" I asked.

"He'll have to stay behind as well," said my mother. Elliott was really mad about this because he wanted to show her his doll and make her **impresstified** by his natural talents. I apologized to Elliott **ten thousandteen** times, but he went to bed mad.

When I woke up on Sunday, I went into the kitchen, where my parents and Magoo were eating breakfast. Everyone was still upset with me because I only got a very soft "Good morning." And not even one "How did you sleep?"

Elliott came out and rubbed the sleep from his eyes. When he opened them, he looked at me and said, "I'm still a little mad at you."

That gave me a bad feeling, but I understood.

"Sorry, Elliott," I said again.

"Okay, kids," my dad said,

clapping his hands together. "We have a very big morning upon us. Elliott and Frannie, we need to hop to it. I need the two of you to vacuum the floors and the couches. When I leave to pick up the toy store woman, I need you to shut Hester, Lester, Esther, and Bark up tightly in the television room. Okay?"

We nodded.

"Mom is going to pick up some nice sandwiches for Magoo's big meeting. While we're gone, I want you to take care of Magoo. Wait on her hand and foot, okay? Whatever she needs or wants, you get it for her. Understand?"

At least we still had jobs to do. Which meant it wasn't too late to show how responsible I was.

Then we got to work. Elliott and

I held the long hose of the vacuum cleaner with all of our hands just to make it steady. It took **forty million hours** to get the cat hair off everything. Once we did that, we had to clean the entire floor!

When we were done, Elliott and I were out of all our breath. We took a little break, but soon our break turned boring since we couldn't do anything because it might mess up the house.

When my parents left, Elliott and I rounded up all the animals and put them in the television room. It was really hard to get each cat in there because they meowed and slipped away every time we'd go to catch them. Once we got all three cats into the television room, Bark followed them and we shut the door very tightly behind us.

If you can even believe it, things got even **boringer.** Magoo said she was going to do fifteen minutes of a *very quiet* exercise called meditation. That meant she was going to sit very still in her meditation room, and we had to be **very, very quiet.** Sitting still did not sound like exercise to me.

"You just need to be quiet for fifteen minutes. Do you think you can do that?" Magoo asked.

"Yes!" we told Magoo.

"You can keep the animals company and watch some television quietly. Okay?"

"We'll be very quiet," I told her. Then she crutched her way into the meditation room where she did an exercise that was not an exercise at all.

Elliott and I went into the television room and roamed around for a good channel, which was not very hard to find since Magoo had one hundred thousand channels. We sat back on Magoo's couch and watched a show on Animal Planet. Bark got up and walked over to Hester, Esther, and Lester, and plopped down next to them. That's when I noticed he was walking funny.

"Elliott," I loud-whispered so we didn't break Magoo out of her meditation.

"What?"

"Bark is limping!"

"He is?"

"Yes! Look at the way he's walking."

Bark was now sitting, so I pulled him up to his feet but he just stood there. I pushed him toward Elliott and whisper-shouted, "Bark! Bark! Go to Elliott. Walk to Elliott!"

And after **foreverteen and a day**, he finally made it over to Elliott and then plopped himself down.

"Did you see it?"

Elliott shook his head no.

"Come on, Bark. Let's take a walk and show Elliott how limpish you are." Then I stood and walked around the room very slowly until Bark got up and followed me.

"See it, Elliott?"

"What's it supposed to look like?" Elliott asked, staring at Bark's legs.

"A limp. You know . . ." And then I
limped to show him what a limp looked
like. Elliott scrunched up his face
and got on all fours and watched very
closely as Bark followed me some more.

"Are you sure, Frannie? I don't see
the limp."

"Maybe we have to look closer."
Then I sat down next to Elliott and
patted my lap until Bark came to
me. I picked up his paw and showed
Elliott.

"Do you see the limp now?" I
asked him. He stared really hard
at the paw.

"I . . . I . . . I'm not sure. Maybe."

That's when I understood that
Elliott couldn't see it because he
wasn't a dog veterinarian! But I was
and that's why I had to officially

explain to Elliott what was the matter.

"He has a case of limp paw."

"Is that bad?"

"Yes, it could lead to broken paw."

"Is that worse?"

"It's what Magoo has, but on humans."

"What do we do?"

"Well, since I'm almost a real veterinarian, but not yet, we should probably take him to the real one down the street."

"But I don't think we're allowed to do that," Elliott said.

"Well, how else are we supposed to learn how to fix him if we don't go?"

"I don't know," he answered.

"How will you know how to be my secretary?"

"I don't know," he said again.

"And how in the worldwide of America will I learn how to fix such a bad case of limp paw if we don't go right now so I can learn?"

Elliott scrunched his face up into a thinking expression.

"You're probably right," he said. "It *does* make sense. And parents like when you do learning experience type things."

"Right," I agreed.

"So maybe it's a good idea."

"It's a fantastical idea!" I said, even though it was my idea and it's almost like bragging but not quite to agree that your own idea is fantastical.

"We'll take him to the veterinarian, and by the time Magoo is done with her meditation, Bark will be fixed and we'll be smarter about limp paw and secretary phones."

"How do we get him there with a broken paw?" Elliott asked.

This was such a good question that I did not correct him that it was limp paw and not broken paw.

We were both **stumpified** as to how to get Bark to the veterinarian. We **harrumphed** our faces and scratched our heads until, finally, I knew exactly how to get him there.

I motioned to the corner where Magoo's wheelchair was folded up. Elliott got up and, almost like he was a professional wheelchair opener, he unfolded it perfectly!

Then we tried very hard to get Bark to jump in and sit. He was not the easiest dog in the world to steer. First we just got his front paws on before he jumped off. Then we got his back paws on before he went skidding off. He was just as slippy as the cats! And that's when I got a genius-al idea!

I held up one finger to Elliott, which meant, *wait one minute*! Then, I ran into the living room where we left Magoo's medical bag and I took out the biggest Ace bandage ever.

We decided that the only way Bark would sit in the chair was if Elliott sat on it first.

"Wait!" Elliott whisper-shouted before he got in. "I want to bring my sock doll so I can finish it while we wait!" He went to the couch, grabbed the sock doll and the thread, and stuck them in his front pocket. Then he got into the wheelchair and we managed to get Bark onto his lap and I **wound and wound and wound** the Ace bandage all around them. Then I wheeled them out the front door and onto the sidewalk. I very carefully shut the front door behind us. It wasn't until we were halfway down the block that I realized I forgot to write a note. It was okay, though. We'd certainly be back before Dad and the toy store lady got home.

I pushed Elliott and Bark down the sidewalk, and people smiled and waved at us. Bark was having a great time. Then we rounded the corner and saw a lot more people with their animals waving at us and smiling. **Walking a dog was really fun!**

When we got to the veterinarian's office, we had to ring a little bell that sounded like a bird chirping. Then we were buzzed in. It was too hard to hold the door open and push the chair through at the same time, so someone in the waiting room had to come out and help us.

I wanted to tell the secretary that we were here, but there wasn't anyone sitting at the front desk.

The waiting room was filled with so many people and animals, it looked like a circus! But I knew it was worth it for me to wait. Once we saw the doctor and he agreed that Bark had limp paw, my family would be so **impresstified**, they would forget all about the crutch incident. Everyone would see what a natural I was with dogs, and they would let me quit school to become a veterinarian!

CHAPTER 10

Since there were no seats left in the waiting room, I wheeled Bark and Elliott to the corner near a plant. Then I tried to memorize every detail of the veterinarian's office so I could copy it at my practice veterinarian's office at home.

A teenage boy holding a soda can looked over at us.

"Cool wheelchair," he said.

Elliott and I looked at each other and smiled. We never really had teenagers talk to us ever. And we never had one tell us we were cool.

"Thanks," I said. "He can't walk because of his limp paw," I explained.

"Totally cool," said the teenage boy.

What a good day this was turning out to be!

"It's not so comfortable," Elliott said to the teenager. He and Bark were still Ace bandaged into the wheelchair. He looked up at me. "Can we get out?"

"I guess so," I said. I untied the back end of the Ace bandage and unwound and unwound. Then, when it was totally unwound, the front door opened and a woman with two dogs

came into the office. I giggled
a little on the inside of my
brain because the dogs looked
exactly like each other.

I guess Bark loves dogs that
look exactly like each other
because that was when he jumped
out of Elliott's lap and raced right
for the door. The dogs got very
scared, even though I know
for a **scientific fact** that Bark
just wanted to play with them.

Suddenly, a **shriekish** type of
sound came from each of the dogs at
exactly the same time. Their owner
pulled back on the leashes, but
Bark went barreling right toward
them! On the way, he knocked into
the other animals and also the
people sitting there waiting to see

the veterinarian.

A woman had her newspaper knocked out of her hands. The teenage boy who had talked to us got his soda knocked out of his hand, and the brown liquid landed in splats all over his jeans.

Rabbits and cats pawed and scratched at their cages, and we could hear loud flapping bird wings and a **millionteen** squawk-squawk-squawks. It sounded like a big waiting room storm. Elliott and I stood there **stumpified** for one second. Then I figured out that since we were the ones Bark came with, we were the ones who had to find him and stop the **hurricane of craziosity**.

"Bark!" I yelled, and then went

to look down the hall, where I heard
even more squawking and barking
and meowing and even human voices

yelling, "Where's the
dog's owner?" "Has
anyone seen my
rabbit?"
"Here, kitty, kitty."
"Someone's going to
pay for this!"
    I was in so much
trouble!

Finally, Bark ran out of one room and across the hall into another. Elliott and I ran toward that room, and as soon as we got there, Bark ran out and into another. He was being really wild and running so fast we couldn't catch him. Then Bark ran into a room and Elliott and I stopped in our tracks when we heard the clanking sound of tools being dropped and things crashing to the floor. It was not the best moment of the world, and that is not an opinion.

A doctor ran out of his doctor room and shouted, "What on earth is going on?! Who is responsible for this animal?"

Elliott and I didn't know what to do because we weren't really responsible for Bark **although at this very exact moment in time we probably scientifically were**. So, finally, I raised my hand very slowly and in a very quiet mouse voice, I said, "I am."

The doctor was calming Bark down with a treat and petting him. Bark was being on his best behavior now. Then a secretary walked out of a different doctor room and stood over us.

"And who, exactly, is responsible for you?"

"Dan and Anna Miller," I told them.

"Well, can you please tell us how to get in touch with them?" The secretary seemed very, very angry. As I told her my mom's cell phone number, I started to get a **very bad-day feeling** on my skin.

"Why don't you wait on the bench outside while I call your mother, okay?" the angry secretary said.

Elliott and I looked at each other with big, worried faces. Then Elliott took Bark by the leash and I followed them into the waiting room, where I got the wheelchair and we headed out the front door. But before we left, I turned to everyone in the waiting room and said sorry to the ground, even though it was meant for the people.

When we got outside, Elliott got back into the wheelchair, we got Bark on his lap, and I wrapped them with the Ace bandage. Then, just as I was about to sit on the bench in front of the veterinarian's office, my mom rounded the corner with a **very bad-day mood** on her face.

And just as she went to open her mouth to let us know how much trouble we were in, her cell phone rang.

"Hello? What? No! Oh my! That's just—Okay, okay, okay. We'll be right there." Then she hung up the phone, looked at us, and said, "Come on kids, we have to hurry!" She raced ahead, rounded the corner, and ran to the end of the block where Magoo lived.

I pushed Bark and Elliott very quickly but also very professionally around the corner and up the block behind my mother. It was **exhaustifying**. By the time we got to Magoo's house, my chest was all out of breath.

Just as my mom was about to open the front door, it flew open and a very large woman with tears in her very red eyes, a swollen face, and red bumps on her neck came running out. Magoo came crutching up to the door behind her yelling, "Wait! Wait! We can do this somewhere else!" And then I saw the slippy cats on the floor behind them.

When I saw the cats, that's when I got a **very bad feeling** in my memory. And that bad feeling was that when I pushed the wheelchair out of the television room, I might have, maybe, perhaps, possibly, it could be, there's a little chance that by the **hugest of accidents**, I left the door just a little bit open.

Maybe.

The big lady stopped when she saw us. I looked behind her and saw Magoo and Dad's bright red, angry faces. My mom was standing next to us, and her face was angry, too.

Elliott and I froze like Popsicles. The lady stood right over us, with her hands on her hips. And we stared up at her, terrified. But then, she did the weirdest thing in the entire world.

She laughed.

I didn't know what she thought was so funny. Looking at all the very mad faces glaring at us from inside Magoo's house, you'd think there'd never be anything funny ever again.

"Who are you and what in the world are you doing?" she asked.

"I'm Frannie and this is my best

friend, Elliott. And that's Bark. We thought he had a case of limp paw, so we took him to the veterinarian around the corner."

"And you brought him in a wheelchair?"

"He had limp paw! He couldn't walk!" Elliott said.

"What's that you have there?" the lady asked, pointing to Elliott's pocket. He looked down and pulled out his sock doll.

"This is my sock doll."

"Did Margot make that for you?"

"No, I'm making it."

"*You're* making it?"

"Yes. And when it's done, it's going to be my good luck charm."

The woman didn't say anything for a minute. Then she turned around and looked at Magoo with brand-new eyes and asked, "Is there a drugstore nearby?"

"Just across the street from the vet's office," Magoo told her.

The lady looked at me and Elliott and asked, "Can you take me there?"

We looked at my dad, who shrugged.

"Okay," I said.

Then the lady turned to Magoo and said, "You put the cats away. I'm going to get some allergy medicine, then I'll come back. I think these children just gave me a marvelous idea about your dolls."

Elliott and I left Bark and the wheelchair with Mom, Dad, and Magoo. They all looked half confused and half the maddest I've ever seen them in my worldwide life and that is very, extremely, professionally mad.

We each took one of the lady's hands and went to the drugstore. She picked out some medicine and also some eyedrops. As soon as she put the drops in her eyes, the red magically disappeared. She told us the splotches and bumps would go away about twenty minutes after she took the other medicine. Then we headed back to Magoo's to hear her *marvelous* idea.

CHAPTER 11

When we got back, my parents had on their "you are in the hugest amount of trouble but we are in front of company so you are not getting punished at this exact minute" expressions.

They had to keep these expressions for a long time since the fancy lady wanted me and Elliott to stay and hear her *marvelous* idea. She gave a long, boring talk about the dolls and said words that had *Q*s in them, so we knew whatever they meant was complicated.

Then she said things about other dolls and other toys, and even though she was talking about dolls and toys, I can tell you for a **scientific fact** that it was **not** interesting. But when she started talking about me and Elliott, suddenly it became interesting.

"When I saw these kids and that little boy with his handmade doll, I had a vision."

Magoo was leaning in so closely, I saw the little hairs on my arms rise and fall from her breath.

"Not only are we going to sell your dolls, but we're going to do workshops where we teach children how to knit, crochet, sew, and . . . with your permission, make your sock dolls."

Magoo inhaled the biggest breath of happiness.

"Really?" she asked.

"Yes, really. I know that the children will love it!" Then she said things that sounded like this: *Boring boring boring. Even more boring. The boringest of boring. Something so boring it bores even the most boring things in the entire world.* **One last thing that is so boring, I just bored my own self to sleep.** I'd like to start as soon as possible. Do you think you could have one hundred dolls in the store by September?"

"Absolutely. It would be my honor," Magoo said.

The fancy toy store woman stood, shook hands with Magoo, gave me and Elliott each a big kiss, and thanked us. And then Mom, Dad, and Magoo

walked and crutched their way to the door. When they came back, Elliott and I stood up, very happy and on our way to play in the other room. My dad put his arm out and rested it on my shoulder.

"Not so fast, Frances."

CHAPTER 12

We were in a **Frances** amount of trouble. When my parents use my full name, Frances, **it's serious**.

We didn't know that we had left the door open behind us when we went to get the wheelchair. So we didn't know that the cats got out, and that Magoo couldn't get them back in the room because she was on crutches. We also didn't know that time went by so fast. What we did know was that we left the house without an adult and that we were just *very* lucky that the fancy toy store lady had a **genius-al** brain and got a good idea just from seeing Elliott with that doll.

We had so much to fix in order to make things right again that I almost lost track.

First, we had to apologize to Magoo. We went into Magoo's room, and she was sitting on her bed, making a brand-new sock doll.

"Magoo?" I said.

"Mmmmm . . . ?" she replied with a needle clamped between her teeth.

"Elliott and I wanted to tell you that we're sorry we almost ruined your life."

Magoo looked up with a smile, but didn't say anything back.

"We were only trying to help because we thought that Bark had limp paw."

"Well, it's nice that you wanted to pitch in, but it sure did cause me a lot of stress," Magoo said.

"I'm sorry."

"I know you are, honey. I would just ask that, in the future, you'll think long and hard before you make a decision. Because if your decision affects other people in a bad way, maybe it's not a good decision."

I looked down at the ground. "Does that mean I was selfish?"

"I'm afraid so," she said.

"I'm sorry, Aunt Magoo. I really didn't mean to be selfish on purpose. I got excited."

"Oh, it's okay, as long as you

learned from it for next time. Now come here, both of you." We went over to Magoo, and she wrapped us up in her arms and hugged us. When we were walking out of the room, she stopped us and we turned around.

"Thank you," she said.

"For what?" I asked.

"For being you. After all, none of this would have happened if it hadn't been for the two of you."

Elliott and I shrugged. Who else were we supposed to be?

Then Dad walked us over to the veterinarian's office, where we apologized to everybody and stayed for one entire hour helping them clean up. I was very worried that we had scared all the animals for the rest of their worldwide lives.

But the secretary said they were all going to be fine, **and that is not an opinion.**

When everything was cleaned up, the secretary showed Elliott how to work the phone bank since he was going to be a veterinarian's secretary. And the veterinarian let me try on his stethoscope and white jacket! It was all **very official** and **definitely** and **clearly professional.**

When we got home, my mom said that even though we had made a lot of apologies, saying we were sorry was not enough. What else in the **worldwide of America** could we do, I wondered?

First, we were not allowed to watch any more TV. We had to go to bed one half hour earlier and read to ourselves instead of being read to. *And* we had to give Hester, Esther, and Lester baths. And if you think cats are slippy when they're dry, you should never wash a cat!

It was the worst day of my entire life, but it was also the best. I was with my best friend in the world, I got to wear a real veterinarian's jacket and a stethoscope, my aunt sold her dolls, and Elliott's sock doll was already lucky charmed!

Everything worked out in the end.

Except that I was not allowed to quit school and become a veterinarian.

Not yet, anyway.

THE END.

FRANKLY, FRANNIE

Check, Please!

by AJ Stern • illustrated by Doreen Mulryan Marts

For Puggy, my grandmother,
who always takes me to fancy restaurants!—AJS

Thanks as always to everyone at Penguin: Francesco
Sedita, Bonnie Bader, Caroline Sun, Christine Duplessis,
Scottie Bowditch, Kimberly Lauber, Jordan Hamessley,
Meagan Bennett, and my editor, Judy Goldschmidt. Your
support and enthusiasm is unparalleled! To Julie Barer,
of course, and her assistant, William Boggess. To my
family and friends for their support.—AJS

CHAPTER

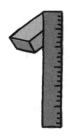

It is a scientific fact that my school fair happens once a year. I wish it happened **twentyteen** times a year, but my dad says "You can't have it all," and that is not an opinion.

The reason my school fair is so fantastical is that they let **all** the students work there! And if you don't already know this about me, I'm a **really** jobbish kind of person. A for instance of what I mean is that I would like a job with an office.

The job at the school fair is not in an office. It's in the cafeteria, but that's okay because it's still a job. The job is called *Spaghetti Lunch*. Spaghetti Lunch is where volunteers from Chester High School make **spaghetti** and the middle-school kids serve it. I am in elementary school, so my job is to pass out **bread and water**. That's certainly a good job because the water comes in a professional-looking pitcher and the bread comes in an official-looking basket.

The morning of the fair, my best friend Elliott and I were so excitified, we could hardly sit still in the back of the car. My mom looked at us in the rearview mirror and smiled.

"You're like a couple of monkeys back there," she teased. "What are you so happy about?" she asked.

"Spaghetti Lunch," I sang.

"And Grab Bag," Elliott added. I nodded, because I agreed with this. **Grab Bag** is where you reach your hand into a big bag that is filled with foreverteen prizes. When you pull out your prize, you are so **excited** because you don't know what's coming.

The moment you see the prize you grabbed is the exact moment you remember that you've always wanted that prize! A for instance of what I mean is that one year I grabbed **candy lipstick**. It wasn't until after I pulled it out that I remembered I had always wanted candy lipstick! You always feel lucky at Grab Bag, and that is not an opinion.

"I'm excited for the raffle this year," my mom told us as she drove into the school parking lot. A raffle is where someone pulls out a name from a jug. Whoever's name is chosen **wins the prize**. "They're raffling off a free dinner at the new restaurant, Balloo," my mom continued. Elliott and I were not so interested in this prize. We were interested in getting to the fair, which is why my mom dropped us off **exactly** in front of the school doors before she looked for a parking space.

"I hope they don't close the raffle before I get there," she said as Elliott and I jumped out of the car. Then my mom leaned over toward the passenger side window and called after me. "Now behave yourself, Mrs. Miller," she said, making one eyebrow go up a step.

"I will!" I yelled as Elliott and I ran up the school stairs and pulled open the front doors. We were so **overwhelmified** by what we saw, our faces almost fell off our heads. There were tables set up with lemonade and face paint and books and games and prizes and a foreverteen amount of things to do. I wanted to do **all of them** at the exact same time.

"Last call for the raffle," my sort-of friend Millicent's mom called out. Millicent is only my sort-of friend because she likes to read books more than she likes to talk to real, live people, like me. Her mother is the head of the Parents' Association, which is why she's in charge of the **raffle**. "Last call before we close!"

I tugged on Elliott's hand. "Come

on. We have to write my mom's name down," I told him.

Elliott and I went over to the raffle table and found the big jug that read: DINNER AT BALLOO. I did not understand why the restaurant was not called *Balloon*. Maybe they ran out of *n*'s? Then I saw that the raffle cost one dollar, and we had exactly **no dollars!** That is when I got an idea. I walked over to Millicent's mom and said, "Excuse me." Sometimes I get embarrassed to "Mr." or "Mrs." someone.

Millicent's mom looked down at me and said, "Hi, Frannie! Do you need me?"

"Well . . . Elliott and I don't have any money. We were wondering if we could make you an IOU for exactly one dollar," I asked her. "And when my mom comes, we can give it to you?"

"That's a great idea, Frannie," she said. I was very **proud** of my great idea. My dad is the one who gave me the idea about IOUs. They're really special because if you say the letters out loud they sound like the words: *I. OWE. YOU.* Sometimes my dad writes them for me if he has to miss my bedtime because of work. They go like this: *IOU one extra-long good-night story!*

Since Elliott's handwriting is very **perfect**, I had him write the IOU and my mom's name on the raffle card. Then I handed Millicent's mom the **IOU**, folded up the card, and dropped her name inside the big jug.

Our job wasn't starting yet, so we decided we would go from table to table until it was ten minutes later.

We guessed how many jelly beans

were in a cookie jar. I guessed **421** and Elliott guessed **422**. We had our fortunes told. Elliott is going to be a fireman and I'm going to work in a real office! *And* I'm going to have an **assistant**, which is the exact thing I want for Christmas!

Finally, it was exactly **noon o'clock** and Elliott and I went downstairs to start our job. I secretly hoped we would get to wear **uniforms**. Uniforms are very extremely grown-up.

CHAPTER

You will not believe what our
class got to wear for Spaghetti Lunch.
Aprons! And they weren't the baby
kind that you have to tie behind your
back AND your neck. They were the
kind you just tie around your waist.

Elliott's babysitter, Tenley, was
the boss of Spaghetti Lunch. She
was volunteering with her friends from
Chester High. Tenley is very serious
about food. She thinks being healthy

is very important and she really hates **sugar**, which is something I never knew a person could hate. But she is very nice, *and* she is in twelfth grade, which is the oldest grade of all. She waved when she saw us, in front of the entire school! Because she was the boss of Spaghetti Lunch AND in twelfth grade, we felt twicely important.

Our teacher, Mrs. Pellington, stood with Tenley at a table next to the kitchen door and clapped to get our attention. Then she explained how to do our jobs, exactly.

"No table should be empty. A good waiter or waitress makes sure every table has bread and water on it."

That was when Tenley made an *I just remembered something I need to tell everyone* face.

"Also, a good waiter or waitress always washes their hands before the beginning of food service, so if anyone hasn't done so yet, now would be the time," she announced. It is a scientific fact that germs are not healthy, which is why Tenley is very serious about clean hands.

A few kids went into the kitchen to use the sink, but not me and Elliott. When Tenley saw us headed in that direction, she took out her wipes and gave one to each of us. That was the third way she made us feel important!

"Remember," Mrs. P. told us when everyone came back from washing their hands, "when you see someone coming with a plate of spaghetti, move out of the way. The plates are very hot. Plus, we don't want anyone to trip and spill spaghetti **all over the place**. And under no circumstance are you to serve anything but bread and water. Is that understood?" Mrs. P. asked us. We nodded our heads.

"Frannie?" she asked me.

I quickly turned my head away from Tenley, who was blobbing **slippy piles of spaghetti** onto the plates.

"Do *you* understand?" Mrs. P. asked in a voice that said *you'd better understand*.

I looked Mrs. P. right in her eyeballs and nodded. This told her I was paying **strict** attention.

"It is a scientific fact that I understand," I told her. And that is when the first customer came into the cafeteria! Soon there was another customer, and then another, until there were a machillion of them. And they all looked very hungry. I brought water and bread to **every** single table. Sometimes the customers were parents and other times they were teachers. I got so good at my job that I even offered to pour the water for my customers. Only one customer said yes, but then she changed her mind when I lifted the pitcher and my hand started to **wobble**.

Soon everyone had their bread and water and things got **boring**. Our job now was to wait. Even though I am a good waiter, I am not good at waiting. Elliott and I waited together, but even then I felt really fidgety. That is why I decided to walk around and see if everyone had all the bread and water that they would ever need in their entire lives.

Over in the corner, I saw a really **teenaged** girl customer sitting by herself waiting for spaghetti. I knew she was waiting because she kept looking at the kitchen with a *where is my spaghetti??* face.

She was looking all around like she was trying to get someone's attention. Then she caught my eye and pointed behind me. I turned to look but didn't see what she was pointing at. When I turned back she was pointing **even harder**, if you can believe that. I turned around again and, behind the older kids, I saw waiting plates of spaghetti. OH! She wanted me to get her a plate of spaghetti!

I felt so much pride-itity that she chose me to be her waitress. I walked over to the counter where all the plates of spaghetti were sitting and I saw the exact **perfect** one. The plate was almost overflowing with spaghetti and steam was floating off the top. For a hungry customer, this was certainly the best choice. I walked right up to it and because I am **really smart** about when to use one hand or two, I picked the plate up with both hands. It was only when I turned around and took some steps toward the teenaged girl that I noticed a really bad feeling on my hands. And less than a centimeter of a second later I realized what the bad feeling was. The plate was boiling-its-head-off hot. I was too **shocktified** to move, but I had to do something with the plate.

Mrs. P. was rushing over to me, and right behind her, I saw my mom.

I don't know how she ended up in exactly the part of the cafeteria where I was doing **a bad thing**. I hadn't even seen her come into school when she was finished parking the car.

Before I even knew what in the whole wide world of America was happening, the very hot plate **flung** out of my hands. Then, like it was in slow motion, I watched the tomato-sauced spaghetti fly across the air and plop in a **splat** all over Mrs. P.'s nice white shoes and the bottom of her white pants.

"Frannie!" my mom shouted, crashing her palm against her forehead.

That is when the entire world stopped breathing, and the whole cafeteria, including the really teenaged girl, turned to stare at me.

My face turned tomato sauce red.
Mrs. P. was staring at her feet. It was
horrendimous. I have never been so
humilified in my whole life, and that
is not an opinion.

"I . . . I . . . The plate was very hot,"
I tried to explain.

"That's exactly why you were not
supposed to touch it!" Mrs. P. said,
raising her voice a little bit.

"I'm sorry, Mrs. P.," I told her. "I'll
help you clean up."

"I think you've done enough already,
Frannie," Mrs. P. said in her *you stay
right where you are, young lady* voice.

My mom was already on the floor
with some paper towels, and Tenley
came rushing out with **a mop**. I did
not even want to turn and see what
Elliott's expression looked like.

"Mrs. P., I am so sorry," my mom said. "I insist that you send me the bill for the cleaning."

"Oh, that's okay," Mrs. P. told her. "I never wear my good things to school, anyway."

"Nevertheless," my mom began (*nevertheless* is a really grown-up word I have to remember to use more oftenly), "why don't you go wash up and I'll take over for you."

"You wouldn't mind?"

"Of course not. It's the least I can do."

Then Mrs. P. turned to me and said, "Frannie, I'm afraid that I'm going to have to ask you to sit out the rest of Spaghetti Lunch." That is when my mouth almost fell down to my own shoes. I looked at my mom.

"That's a very lenient punishment,

Frannie," my mom explained.
Lenient meant "that's not a very
bad punishment at all!" I knew the
word *lenient* from the last time I was
punished, which was exactly not so
long ago.

Mrs. P. pointed to a very strict chair
in the most **boring** section of the
cafeteria. It was all the way off in the
corner where nothing ever happened!

"And I'd like you to think about the
difference between good helping and
bad helping. Is that clear?"

I nodded my head yes.

"Okay, Mrs. P.," I said. "I'm
sorry about your shoes and pants. I
really am. I will go think about some
differences now in the boring area."
And that is when I **slunked** my way
over to the bad section. I sat there for

three months and forty hundred years. Mrs. P. came back from the bathroom all cleaned up, but with spaghetti stains. Then she clapped **twice** to get our attention.

"Okay, class, let's line up and take a bow, because we did such a great job!"

I love bows! I jumped right out of my **boring seat** and ran over to stand next to Elliott. And that is when the second most horrendimous thing happened. Mrs. P. turned to me and said in a really strict way, "Frannie, please go back to your seat. I'll tell you when it's time to get up."

I could not in a millionteen years **believe** this! Elliott's mouth almost fell off his face at the same time as mine. I was shocktified. I did not know that punishments were **more important than bows**.

I slunked back to my chair and watched my entire class take a really important bow **without me**. I could tell that Elliott was upset that I wasn't next to him. I knew because he didn't bow as hard as I've seen him bow in the past. The whole world of the cafeteria clapped for the good job my class did. I love getting claps, but I didn't do a good job, so I didn't get any. I was very angrified at myself for spilling **hot spaghetti** all over Mrs. P.'s clothes. I was never going to touch a hot plate ever again. Not in a machillion years.

CHAPTER

My mom was still upset with me
when it was time for the **raffle**. She
was a really fancy kind of mad: She was
cross. Cross is worse than angry because
I don't really know what it means.

We settled into our seats in the
auditorium, and Elliott and I jittered
our legs with excitement. I felt my belly
fill up with **moths and butterflies**.
Even though I was being crossed at,
I still wanted my mom to win the raffle.

She didn't know that Elliott and I put her name in the big jug. She also didn't know we owed Millicent's mom **one dollar**, but I would tell her later. If she won then she'd be less grumpy and maybe she'd uncross herself at me.

There was a lot of chattering, and then soon everyone went really quiet. Millicent's mom came on the stage carrying a big jug with millions of papers stuffed inside it. Millicent stood next to her. For once her head was not in a book. Maybe Millicent loves her mom more than she loves books.

Then, before the big raffle for the families, Millicent's mom held up the **jelly bean jar** that we guessed at.

"We had a lot of very fine guesses, but no one guessed the exact number," she told us. That sentence got a big groan. "There are 409 jelly beans in here. The person with the closest guess was only twelve jelly beans off. At 421, our winner is Frannie B. Miller! Frannie, please come to the stage and collect your prize!"

It is a scientific fact that I had never won anything before. I was so **nervous** to go up on the stage alone that I grabbed Elliott's hand and made him come with me.

"Congratulations," Millicent's mom said into the **microphone** as she handed me the extremely heavy jar.

"Thank you for your congratulations," I said back into the microphone. Then added, "Elliott guessed 422, so I'm going to share this with him." And that was when the crowd applauded, **actually**.

Can you even believe that fact? Not only was I the winner of 409 jelly beans, but I was **the winner** of clapping! It certainly made up for losing out on Spaghetti Lunch clapping!

Then Millicent's mom announced that it was time for the big dinner raffle, and Elliott and I went back to our seats. She made it sound like getting to eat at the Balloon restaurant was the **best** part of the entire raffle, but it's a scientific fact that it was not.

Someone in the audience made a **drumroll** sound. Millicent's mom stuck her hand in the jug. After feeling around for nearly fifty hours, she pulled out a piece of paper.

And you'll never believe what I'm about to tell you: *That* piece of paper she pulled out looked EXACTLY like the white piece of paper Elliott wrote my mom's name on. It took her thirty-seven hours to unfold the piece of paper and a century before she read it out loud.

"Well, what do you know!" she said in a *what a coincidence!* voice. "The winner of the dinner raffle is none other than Anna Miller, Frannie Miller's mother!" Everyone in the audience clapped. I looked over at my mom, whose face was bright red and twisted in a confusified expression. And that's when I gave her my big *that's right, I entered you in the raffle while you were trying to find a parking space* smile. She gave me a very big smile back and grabbed my hand. "That was a very thoughtful thing to do, Bear," she whispered in my ear as she led me back to the stage.

That was when my **heart** almost exploded out of my own chest.

Onstage, my mother collected the gift certificate and then said thank you into the microphone, and we went back to our seats. Then she whispered to me, "It's a *French* restaurant!"

Two seconds before I didn't even care about eating at

a fancy restaurant, but now I couldn't wait. That was when I squeezed my mom's hand, which told her in no words how excitified I was, nevertheless.

CHAPTER 4

That night at dinner I showed my dad the big jar with my half of the **jelly beans**. Showing my dad was one of the hugest mistakes of my career because he acted just like he did with Halloween candy. I was allowed to **scoop** out one handful, and then he'd hold on to the rest until I was allowed another scoop. It is a scientific fact that I planned on **scooping** out the best handful

of jelly beans ever, and that is not
an opinion. Plus, I was also going to
hide beans all around the house so
that they would last forever.

After my dad put the jelly bean jar
away, me and my mom told him all
about the fair, my IOU (which my mom
paid back), and even the part about the
spaghetti on Mrs. P.'s shoes.

"But I already got in trouble about
that," I told him, in case he wanted to
punish me about it all over again.

"Did you get a fair punishment?"
he asked.

"Yes!" I said, and very quickly changed
the subject before he and my mom had
a chance to send **brain messages** to
each other that my punishment really
was too lenient.

"And Mom won a raffle!"

My dad looked at her and she gave him the hugest smile.

"You'll never guess what it was," she said.

"A new car?" Dad asked.

"Nope," Mom answered.

Dad tried again. "A new house?"

"Nope," Mom said.

"Fourteen billion dollars?" he tried one last time.

Then Mom leaned in, put her hand on his, and said, "Dinner at Balloo." It is a scientific fact that dinner at Balloon is not better than **fourteen billion dollars**, but the way my mom said it made it seem like it was.

"Well, I'll be!" my dad said, slapping his hand down on the table.

"The chef is supposed to be amazing," my mom told him. "But I haven't seen a word about it from any of the food critics."

"It might be too early for them to send a food critic," my dad said.

What in the worldwide of America were they talking about?

"What's a food critic?" I asked.

"A food critic is someone who eats at restaurants and writes about the food and the service."

"Is this a real, live, actual job?" I asked.

"Yes, it is," my mom told me.

"Do food critics have offices?"

My parents looked at each other with **question mark faces**.

"I think they probably write in an office, yes," my mom said.

In my entire life as a person, I had never heard about people eating for their actual job. Being a food critic sounded like the most **spectacular job** in the worldwide of America.

It was very easy to picture myself as a food critic. I saw myself sitting alone, in the middle of a long, **rectangular** table, while waiters put one plate of food after another in front of me. The customers were all turned to face me, like an audience at the theater, and everyone was very quiet while I chewed. After every bite, I announced to the restaurant what I thought about the food, and all the eaters would **ooh** and **ahhh** and maybe even clap.

But then I was a little stumpified.

"But how do you describe the taste of food?"

"Well, take this soup for example.

Why don't we all have a sip and describe the taste to one another?" my mother suggested.

My dad, mom, and I scooped up a big spoonful of the most **delicious** vegetable soup that my dad made.

My mom said, "This soup is comforting and reminds me of sitting in front of the fireplace with my two favorite people."

My dad said, "To me the soup tastes light and airy, not too watery, salty but flavorful, and it hits the spot."

And then I said, "It tastes like carrots, celery, zucchini, and clear broth." I looked down at the soup to make sure I wasn't leaving anything out, and then quickly added, "And rice!"

My parents smiled because they knew I was **exactly right**.

"Good job, Frannie," my dad said, and I smiled from one side of our house to the other. I *loved loved loved* when my dad Good-Job-Frannie'd me.

I took another sip, and they looked at me and waited. It was just like I imagined it would be at the restaurant where I was working as a **food critic**. I swished it around in my mouth and chewed on all the vegetables, swallowed, and then looked up at the ceiling until I had the **perfect** description.

"The taste I taste is a soupy taste," I told them with a very professional voice.

"That's a good start, Bird," my dad said.

My dad is the only person who calls me that. It is a scientific fact that **Bird** is my middle name, but please do not tell anyone.

"Vegetable soupy," I added.

When I saw the pride-itity on my dad's face after I said *vegetable soupy*, I knew right then and there I was meant to be a food critic.

CHAPTER 5

After school the next day, my mom and I were sitting on the living room floor making a **scrapbook** together. We were very concentratey, which

is why we both did shoulder jumps when my dad came through the front door.

"I have some very interesting news!" my dad said as he put down his briefcase.

"What? Tell us!" my mom said.

"Maria Cross *might* be going to Balloo the same night we're going!" he said. And then before I could even ask the question out loud, he turned to me and answered it: "She's the food critic at the *Chester Times*!"

This was a for instance of when my brain thinks two things at the exact same time. The first thought was: *If Cross were my last name, I would make sure everyone in the entire world knew it was a* last name *kind of cross, not an* I'm mad at you *kind of cross.*

The **second brain thought** made me stand up and ask out loud, "Food critics are famous?!"

"Some are, yes," said my dad. "But Maria Cross is the *most* famous. In Chester, at least."

"How do you know where Maria Cross is going to be?" my mom asked.

"Well, I was in line at the grocery store when the woman behind me took a call. She was whispering, as if she didn't want anyone to hear, but she was *right* behind me, so it was hard *not* to. Anyway, I heard her say something like, 'Maria's going to Balloo either this Friday or next.' "

My mom **scrunched** her face and thought about this for a second.

"How do you know the woman on the phone was talking about Maria

Cross? Couldn't she have been talking about a different Maria?"

"Good question," said my dad. I could tell that whatever he was about to say actually filled him with **pride-itity**. "I know because the woman mentioned Maria's newspaper the very next time she spoke. She said something like, 'That's how they do it at the *Chester Times . . .*'"

I looked at my mom to see if she was **convinced**.

"Hunhhh . . . ," she said, which meant that she was! (I'm very smart about whether my mom is convinced.)

"Wow. Can we get there early for a front-row seat?" I asked.

Now my parents scrunched their faces at *me*!

"Front-row seat? We're going to a restaurant, Birdy, not the theater," said my dad. "Plus, she also might *not* be going this Friday night, when we're going. She might be going *next* Friday."

They certainly didn't know as much about restaurants as I thought they did.

"But we still have to be up close so we can hear what she says," I explained. "Then we'll know what's good and bad and order all the right things!"

My parents were silent for exactly one-half of a second before they both **laughed out loud**.

"That's not exactly how it works," my mom said, once she stopped laughing.

I sat back down, disappointed.

"Well then, how *does* it work?" I asked.

"First of all, the restaurants aren't

supposed to know that the critic is there because the critic doesn't want **special** service," she said.

"Why not?" This **confused** me. I didn't know anyone who didn't like special service.

"Because a critic's job is to tell people what to expect when they visit a restaurant. But if the chef puts more care into preparing the critic's food, then the food described by the critic isn't the same food everyone else gets to eat," my mom explained.

I thought about that for a second until my brain decided it **made sense**.

"So how does it work, exactly? If no one knows the famous food person is there, then how does the famous food person get any food?" I asked.

"The critic makes a reservation,

just like everyone else. They get their own table and when they get the menu, the fun part begins," my dad explained, adding, "The critic orders as much food on the menu as possible without looking like too much of a pig."

"Sometimes they bring friends so it doesn't look weird that one person is ordering everything on the menu," my mom said.

My dad leaned back. "Then, when they're done, they write an article about everything they experienced. And then the newspaper publishes it."

That is when I got the most **spectacular** idea. "Can we invite Elliott to Balloon?" I asked.

My parents looked at each other. Sometimes this means they are having **brain conversations.**

"Sure we can," my dad said.

"We'll write a review, too."

"What a great idea, Frannie!"

"Which newspaper does Maria Cross put her articles in again?"

"The *Chester Times* of New York."

"Oh! That's *my* newspaper! Remember when I had my picture taken with the new mayor of Chester and it was published in that exact newspaper?" I reminded them.

Since the *Chester Times* already knew who I was, there was a good chance they'd put something I wrote in their paper. Right then I knew I had better write a review I could be **proud** of.

CHAPTER 6

I did not know it was possible to be **nervous** about going to a restaurant, but standing outside Balloon on Friday night, I noticed how many moths and **butterflies** were swimming around my belly. My parents and Elliott were excitified to go inside, but I asked them to wait. I had to check inside my briefcase to make sure that everything I had packed was still there: my résumé (which is a list of all the jobs I've had), my business cards, two pads of stapled-together scrap paper, two pencils, my dad's old pair of glasses with the lenses taken out (he wears contacts now), and an envelope.

I closed my briefcase and nodded to my parents and Elliott to let them know that I was ready. Then we went inside, and you would not even **believe** what we saw. First of all, there were a hundredteen people eating dinner. It was the most crowded restaurant I had ever seen. There were even people standing in the front part of the restaurant waiting to get a table. Music was playing, and there was **clatter** from all the silverware and china and the sound of a hundredteen people talking to one another.

How in the worldwide of America

299

was I supposed to review all this? I didn't think I knew enough words to describe any of it. That's when I got a geniusal **idea**. I turned to Elliott.

"Do you want to describe the restaurant and I'll describe the food?"

Elliott's eyeballs almost popped out of his head.

"Yes!" he said.

"Okay. When we get to our table, I'll give you some paper and a pencil."

I could tell that Elliott was very **happy** I asked him. His face was filled with pride-itity.

When we sat down, I tried to see if there was a lady sitting all by herself who could be Maria Cross, but I didn't see anyone alone. Maybe she wasn't there yet.

One **centimeter** of a second after

we sat down, a waiter in an actual tuxedo came over and gave us the hugest menus I'd ever seen. They were so **heavy** that Elliott and I each had to hold up ours with both of our hands. We were stumpified by the menus. A for instance of what I mean is that the words on the menu were not even in English. They were in French!

Another for instance of why the menu was so **confusifying** was that it didn't have any pictures of what the food looked like. I like seeing **pictures** of the food because if it looks delicious then that's what I point to when the waiter comes over. I also like it when the picture has a number underneath because all you have to remember is the number and not some long, complicated food name.

Like *tortelnoodi* or *spaghettivealinaise*.

Before my mom had a chance to translate the words for me and Elliott, the tuxedo waiter came over, and when he asked if we'd like to hear the specials, my parents said yes.

This was not such a good idea. The waiter bent down so he was closer to our **eardrums** and turned his face channel to very serious. Then he started to tell us about all the different dishes in a very **whispery**, storytelling voice. He went on and on about each little thing in the dish, and I thought he might cry. It was like he was talking about his favorite aunt whom he loved so much, but couldn't see because she lived **far, far, far away in Pennsylvania**.

He told us how everything was

cooked and what everything came with and sometimes he **fluttered** his hands like he was pretend-cooking. Other times he kissed his fingertips and then tossed them up in the air like he was throwing a real, live **kiss** across the room! His accent was already funny, but sometimes he danced the words around when he said them, or stretched them out. Like, instead of saying *little*, he said *leeeeetle*. The worst of it was that he did not stop talking, ever.

Elliott and I couldn't even help ourselves. We were trying not to be obvious about laughing, but our laughing kept making our menus bounce up and down. I tried very hard to think of terrible things so I would **stop laughing**, but it didn't work.

Remember how sad it was when your whole class took a bow at Spaghetti Lunch and you had to sit all by yourself and watch? But even that didn't help me. It made it worse, actually.

Soon, **tears ran down my face**, and my shoulders were shaking up and down at how the serious waiter didn't even know how funny he was. How could my parents keep such straight faces? I looked over at my dad, whose lips turned up at the ends into the teeniest, tiniest **curl smile** (I'm very smart about curl smiles), which is how I knew that he was trying not to laugh. And my mom scrunched her eyes to show she was being very **concentratey**, but I know that she was also trying not to laugh.

Then my dad said, "Thank you. I think we'll need another minute."

When the waiter walked away, Elliott and I dropped our menus, but, instead of **bursting out laughing**, we just sort of . . . stopped. My parents looked at us, both with strict faces.

"What?" I asked with very wide eyes, like I didn't know what I did wrong.

"You know better than to laugh at people," my mom said, being a little bit **scoldish**.

"We weren't laughing at *him*!" I told her. "We were laughing at the way he was talking!"

"That's the same thing. Plus, he was just trying to do his job, and you made him feel bad."

I hung my head down.

"Oh," I said. I hadn't meant to make anyone feel bad. It's just that he was saying all these fancy words in a very serious and **emergency type of way** and it tickled me from the inside, and when you are tickled from the inside, you don't have a choice about laughing. You just HAVE to.

"Sorry," I told her.

"Sorry," Elliott added. I could tell he felt bad, too, because he had worry on his forehead. That's when his forehead gets lots of lines on it from too much **worrying**.

"Good. Now you can apologize to him when he returns."

My Cheerio eyes practically zoomed out of my head.

"*To* him? But he's a stranger!"

"Yes, but you're with us, so it's okay to talk to him," my mom explained.

"Strangers have feelings, too," my dad added.

He was right about that, too, and that gave me a very **bad-day feeling** in my belly. I hated hurting people's feelings, especially grown-up men who were very **serious** about restaurant specials.

When he came back to the table, I looked up at the waiter to apologize. "I'm sorry that we laughed," I said, looking at his eyebrows instead of his **eyeballs** so I wouldn't feel so ashamed.

"I'm sorry, too," Elliott added.

The waiter made a little laugh and said, "You are not the only children who have laughed at my accent."

Even though he gave a little laugh, he did not look happy about this fact.

"I will tell all the children of the world to stop it," I told him in a very serious tone.

"Thank you, mademoiselle," said the waiter, and then he **flipped** open his waiter pad. We gave our orders, and when I was done ordering my spaghetti from the kids' section of the menu, I got up all my bravery to ask the waiter a very important question.

"Excuse me, Mister Waiter . . . ," I said just as he was turning to walk away.

"Yes?"

I stood up so he would understand that the question I was asking was extremely important.

"Can you tell me if the famous restaurant reviewer Maria Cross is here yet?" I was so proud of my **professional** sound that I almost jumped out of my own skin when my parents both gasped.

"Frannie!" my mother shouted.

And my dad snapped, "Bird!"

The waiter and I looked at each other. We were both very confusified at my parents' reactions.

"What?" I asked.

"Remember what we explained to you?" my dad asked.

I shook my head no. My parents explained a **millionteen things** to me. How was I supposed to know the exact thing he was talking about?

My dad looked up at the waiter and said, "She's a little confused. She doesn't really know what she's saying."

The waiter **shrugged**, but had a curious look on his face, like he knew a special secret and was thinking about telling it to other people. I am very smart about **curious** looks and special secrets. After the waiter left, my parents turned back to me.

"First of all, we don't even know whether Maria Cross will be here tonight. She might very well have decided to come next Friday night. But, more importantly, restaurants aren't supposed to know the critics are at the restaurants, remember? So there should be no mention of her name, whatsoever," my dad reminded me.

I slapped my hand against my forehead. "I forgot about that!" I said. And while I did feel really bad about giving away a secret, I had to make a brain note about the word *whatsoever*. It was very **grown-up** and I wanted to use it as oftenly as possible.

CHAPTER

When the waiter came back, he had
a bread basket and a pitcher of water
with him. Just like the ones they had at
Spaghetti Lunch! I looked up at him.

"Remember before how I asked
about the famous restaurant reviewer,
Maria Cross?" I could feel my parents
getting ready to **slam** their hands
against their foreheads.

"Yes . . . ," the waiter said, waiting for
me to tell him a really **special** secret.

"Well, that was a mistake. I thought we were at a different restaurant where Maria Cross is supposed to be—"

"That'll be enough, Frannie," my dad interrupted.

"—but I was wrong about that because we're not at that restaurant. We're at this one. And she's not supposed to be here. Not tonight, or *whatsoever*. Maria Cross, I mean," I said.

For some reason that I did not understand, I could not **stop** talking. I could not stop explaining how Maria Cross wasn't going to be here. I just wanted to talk that expression off his face. The one that said *even though you are saying one thing I still believe the other thing you said earlier.*

And that is the reason why, when he came back to deliver our appetizers, I said, "So you believe me, right? About Maria Cross not being here?"

"Frannie!" my dad finally almost-yelled. I looked at him.

"What?" I asked as the waiter stood there waiting to hear what my dad was going to tell me.

"Enough."

When the waiter walked away, my table was very quiet except for the sound of **water-sipping and bread-chewing**. I looked over and saw him whispering to another waiter, and then I watched as that waiter went into the kitchen, and two minutes later a very sweaty, red-faced man dressed all in white came out and looked around the restaurant.

I knew exactly what they were doing. They were looking for Maria

Cross. My waiter had told! He hadn't **believed** me!

The waiters were looking and looking around until, **all of a sudden**, the big, sweaty man in all white nudged his chin in the direction of a lady, sitting all by herself. She was a very big lady, which made sense since her job was to eat. She had black, **curly** hair and she had something on her lap, which meant she was hiding something. Probably a pad of paper for notes. Even though I couldn't see exactly if I was right, I knew I was.

Maria Cross!

I nudged Elliott with my elbow and threw my eyeballs in her direction. When Elliott saw her, he didn't even have to ask who I was talking about. He knew. Sometimes he doesn't even

have to read the thoughts in my brain.
Sometimes he can just hear them.

I was going to do everything Maria
Cross was going to do.

I looked up at my parents.

"Elliott and I are going to start our
restaurant review now," I told them.

"Okay, just be quiet about it," my
dad said.

"We will."

And then I opened my briefcase and pulled out my two pads and gave one to Elliott. I put mine **on my lap**, like Maria Cross, and Elliott did the same. Then we each held on to our pencils and waited. I knew we both looked very professional. Probably like we should have been in an **office**.

CHAPTER

The thing about restaurant reviews
is that we did not know how to write
them. We had never even read one
before. We were **stumpified**.

Elliott was looking around the
restaurant, and I could see his brain
trying to find words to **describe**
everything. I stared at all the food, trying
to think of words to describe salad. I
looked down at what I had so far:

Salad.

I looked over and saw what Elliott had written down so far:

Crowded.

This was not a good sign. I looked over at Maria Cross. Then I looked at Elliott.

"We have to see what's on her pad," I told him.

Elliott nodded in agreement. Maria Cross would certainly have food descriptions on her pad that would **nevertheless** help us get started. That's when I got a geniusal idea.

"I have to go to the bathroom," I said.

"Me too," Elliott said.

"Go together and wait for each other, please," my mom said with her **face channel** turned to strict.

Maria Cross's table was on the

way to the bathroom. Elliott and I tried to get close so we could see her pad as we passed by. But we got too close because we banged right into her table! Her glass **wobbled,** and she looked up from her lap and made a mad face at us. Suddenly I felt a hand on my shoulder. It belonged to my dad. He leaned over and said to Maria Cross, "I am so sorry about that."

"That's all right," she said in a really high kind of voice.

"You're supposed to be on your way to the bathroom," he said. "Please use it and come right back to our table. Is that understood?"

We said that we did understand and then we walked directly toward the bathroom. Right when we reached the bathroom area, my eyeballs got distractified. The kitchen was *right there*! And we could see exactly right inside it because there was no door!

There were a machillion people **rushing** around in there. Some people were yelling in another language, and other people were cooking a millionteen things at once. There was a long table where waiters put plates with **fancy** food, and also bread baskets and pitchers of water!

Something on one of the plates looked a little weird. I took a couple steps closer. And that is when I saw the most **newsbreaking** story of ever.

I nudged Elliott and pointed toward a plate. When he saw the plate, he almost fainted. You will not in one hundredteen years believe what we saw in that kitchen on that plate.

BUGS!

My eyeballs were not even seeing things wrong. We stepped a little bit closer, and sure enough we saw the little **bug heads** popping out of their bug shells. Then a waiter came over and poured **warm butter** all over them, picked up the plate, and brought it out to serve it to someone!

"Should we tell someone?" I asked Elliott.

"I don't know," he answered.

"Someone is about to eat buttered bugs without even knowing it!"

Elliott just stood there with his eyes bulging out all over the place. He didn't know what to do, either.

We both stuck our heads **back in the kitchen** and nearly fell over when a couple of waiters came running out yelling, "Hot plates, very hot plates!"

"They seem very busy," Elliott said. He was right. I didn't want to interrupt them. So we went back to our table before my dad decided to **arrest us and put us in jail.**

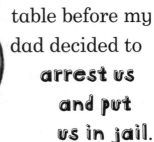

Our main course had already been served. My parents seemed a little **angry** at us. Elliott and I sat down, and I studied our plates for bugs.

"What in the world were you two thinking?" my mother asked as she cut into her chicken.

"We didn't mean to get so close to her table," I explained.

"It just sort of happened that way," Elliott added.

"You need to leave her alone and let her write her review, if that's even what she's doing," my mom said.

I looked at my mom's plate and then at my dad's to make sure there were no bugs on them. There weren't, but I was very **concerned** that someone in the restaurant *would* have bugs on their plate! That is when I got the most fantastical idea. I wrote something down on a piece of notebook paper, ripped it out, and handed it to Elliott.

Let's write a note to Maria Cross and tell her about the bugs!

If anyone could stop people from eating bugs, it was Maria Cross! Elliott read my note and looked at me with **a face** that said *Frannie—you are a genius of the earth.*

I handed Elliott the pad because he has very good handwriting. That is why he is my **secretary**. Then I whispered each sentence to him, and he wrote down every single word I said in the very strictest letters. *We know you are here. We won't tell anyone. We saw a waiter pour butter on a plate of insects and then bring it out to a table. Someone in this restaurant is now eating* a dinner with bugs on their plate. It could be you!

When he was done, he showed it to me and I was very **impresstified** with the way it looked. He was very impresstified with how it sounded. Then I handed it back, and he added:

Thank you,
The Secret People.

I gave him **the most gigantic smile** about that last line. Then I wondered how we were supposed to get this note to her.

"I have to go to the bathroom again," I told my parents.

Elliott looked confused.

"You just went," my dad said.

"I know, but I couldn't go. I need to try again," I said.

"Quickly, please," my dad said.

I got up and brought the pad with me. When I reached the bathroom, I tore the note off the pad of **paper** and folded it in half so no one could read it. Then I **tugged** on a waiter's sleeve, and when he bent down I asked him if he would take the note to someone.

"Who?" he asked me.

I couldn't tell him her name because I wasn't supposed to let anyone know that Maria Cross, famous restaurant reviewer of the world, was here, so I had to point, which I felt bad about because **pointing is rude**.

"Her," I said, pointing to Maria Cross. The waiter nodded and took the note from me. Then, I actually *did* have to go to the bathroom.

The bathroom was very fancy. It

had music playing in it and an **actual waterfall** coming down a wall. There were a lot of different sprays on a shelf, and I sprayed one just to see what it smelled like.

Roses!

The toilet didn't flush by itself like the usual toilets in restaurants did. Instead, this one had a flusher that hung down from the ceiling on a chain. It took me foreverteen minutes to figure out I was supposed to pull it in order to get it to **flush**.

When I went back to our table, I saw the waiter walk over to Maria Cross's table. I nudged Elliott, and we both turned as she opened the note, read it, and then, at the top of her **lungs**, and I am not even making this up, she screamed, grabbed her purse and her coat, and ran out of the restaurant! Everyone stopped eating and watched her. When she got to the door, she **banged** into a lady and looked right in her face and yelled something that sounded like "Bugs!"

Then *that* lady shrieked, ran to her table, and whispered something in her husband's ear. They quickly got up and left, too.

And that is when things started to go not so right.

Suddenly, the customers in the front of the restaurant were **shrieking** and jumping up and yelling for their checks. The waiters and chefs were running out, trying to calm everyone down, but it didn't seem to work because before we even knew it, the front part of the restaurant was **nearly empty**.

My parents looked very confused. My dad turned to my mom. "What did she say?"

"I don't know," my mom answered. "Rugs?"

Then they looked at me and Elliott like we had **something** to do with it!

"What??" I asked them.

"Nothing," my mom said. "Just looking. Can't I just look at you?" she asked with an *I'm not really "just looking"at you, I'm suspicious that you are up to no good* face.

That felt like **a trick question**, so I looked at Elliott, who shrugged, and then I looked back at my parents and said, "I guess so." And then added, "But I don't have to like it one bit!"

CHAPTER

During the car ride home, my dad kept looking at us in the **rearview** mirror. His look asked if Elliott and I did something to make Maria Cross scream and run out of the restaurant. My mom turned around to face us.

"So you have no idea what Maria Cross, if that was even her, said when she ran out?"

Elliott and I shook our heads no. I felt **horrendimous** not telling them

the truth, but I was a restaurant critic
right now and we work in **secret**.
My parents would have to learn
about what happened once it was
in the newspaper. Just like all the
other readers in the world.

It was a really good thing that
Elliott was sleeping over because we
had to write this review as fast as
possible. We had to get it in all the
newspapers so the restaurant could get
an **exterminator** and get rid of

all those bugs. Our parents were going to be so proud of us.

When we got home, Elliott and I rushed up to my desk and pulled two chairs together. He started to write about the restaurant (I told him about the bathroom so he wrote about that, too) and I wrote about the food. Then Elliott rewrote the whole review in his geniusal handwriting.

Tenley was going to babysit me and Elliott the next day. Since she knew about **healthy** things, we thought she should know about the bugs at Balloon. So our plan was to show her our review first.

Here is the review we wrote:

This is a restaurant review of the most awfulest restaurant in the world. It is written by two people: Frannie B.

Miller, who will review the food part, and Elliott Stephenson, who will review the restaurant part.

Tonight we had the most worst meal in the entire city of Chester. We had it at a new restaurant. The new restaurant is really bad first of all because it is called Balloon, but they forgot the letter *n*, so the awning just says Balloo. Also, it was VERY crowded. There were so many people there that we had to give our coats to someone to put away. But the worst, worst, worst thing is what we're about to tell you: It is not an opinion that there were actual insects in the kitchen and the waiter poured butter on them. Then he took that plate and brought it to someone who would eat BUGS in butter, without even knowing it! We wrote Maria Cross a note about this and she did the exact right thing and screamed and ran out of the restaurant!

Then lots of other people screamed and ran out of the restaurant. My parents did not hear what the people were screaming about and so we stayed all the way through to dessert. Then we left and came home to write this review. Thank you for reading this review. the end.

PS: There were some good things we forgot to tell you. The bathroom had a ceiling flusher that you pulled. Also there were sprays that smelled like roses and a waterfall that ran down a wall, which I did not see, but Frannie told me about.

CHAPTER 10

The next morning, we looked at the *Chester Times* because my parents have it **delivered** every day. We were relieved to see that Maria Cross did not write her review there yet. We wanted to be the first ones to review the terrible restaurant, Balloon. I had a very strong feeling in my **heart** that when the newspaper printers read it, they would hire me and Elliott as their new restaurant reviewers.

Tenley came over and said we were going to have a really fun day. Then we all walked into town so we could go to **the hobby store**. The hobby store is where we buy our hobbies. A for instance of what I mean is that sometimes Elliott and I like to tie-dye T-shirts. The hobby store is where we buy the tie-dye T-shirt kits.

On the walk over, we told her all about the bad restaurant and then handed her the **review**. She took the review from our very hands and read it right then and there. We watched her face grow very angrified.

"So the bugs were not crawling on the floor? They were on the plate?"

I nodded. "Yup. They were just right there, dead on a plate."

"In butter," Elliott added.

Tenley moved her face into a *gross* expression.

"You make it sound like there were a lot. It wasn't just one bug? Like a fly that **accidentally** flew onto the plate or something?"

"There were a lot of them. Like sixteen of them!"

"That is really revolting," Tenley said. *Revolting* was a really good word.

"It was *very* revolting," I said.

Tenley thought for a minute. Then she looked back at us and asked, "Are you one hundred percent positive that they were bugs? They couldn't have been anything else? Maybe a type of food that *looks* like bugs?"

"What kind of food looks like bugs?" I asked.

Tenley thought about this for a minute. "Caviar looks like hundreds of ants mushed together in a pile. Is that how they looked?"

I looked at Elliott and passed a brain note to him. It said, "She is not listening to us!" And Elliott sent one back that said, "I know, but I'm not the boss of her, so I can't really do anything about that!" I wondered whether I needed to use my English accent so she would really listen to me. But I decided against it.

"That is not how they looked because, like I just told you, there were about sixteen of them. And also, they were bugs!" I told her this with a face that did not move a muscle and that could only mean one thing: THEY WERE BUGS!

"They were *definitely* bugs," Elliott agreed.

"Well, if you're a hundred percent sure, then we have to do something right away," she said. Then she stared directly into my eyeballs. "Are you a hundred percent sure, Frannie?"

"A hundred percent," I said.

"And, Elliott," she asked, looking directly into his eyeballs, "are you a hundred percent sure, too?"

"A hundred percent," he also said.

"Fine. Then we need to take action now," she said. "This is a very serious health issue."

I hadn't thought about that. It was true that we probably should have told people about the bugs instead of keeping them a secret.

"I have an idea," Tenley said, but

she didn't tell us the idea! She just
walked really quickly, like we were
late to meet her idea.

When we got to the hobby store,
she finally told us what she was
thinking.

"We are going to make signs." I
thought this was a spectacular idea.
We bought all the **supplies**. Then
we sat at a table they had in the hobby
store for making signs just like this.
This is what we wrote in very big
letters:

THERE ARE
BUGS
AT BALLOON.
DON'T EAT HERE!

We made twelve hundredteen signs. Then we walked up and down the street taping our signs to poles, and **marched** right up to the restaurant, Balloon. It was closed because it was daytime, so we taped a sign to the front window.

We stood back and smiled at the good job we had done. When I looked down the street, I saw people already **crowding** around some of the signs and reading them. It was working!

Then, on our way home, we stopped at the **post office**, where Tenley bought us a stamp and an envelope. Tenley showed us how to look up the address for the *Chester Times* in the phone book at the post office. And then, because Elliott is my secretary and has geniusal handwriting, he addressed the letter:

Maria Cross's Boss
The Chester Times
345 Pearl Street
Chester, NY 10758

Elliott and I walked to the post office window and handed the window person our letter. I looked at her in a very strict but **polite** way and said, "It's very important that this go to the newspaper. Thank you very much."

Then she said, "I will personally see to it."

She was taking me very seriously. That felt really grown-up. Another thing that felt grown-up was her **name tag**. I am very interested in name tags. I made a brain note to make one for myself when I got home. Maybe I'd even wear it to school.

CHAPTER 11

When I got home, my parents were in the TV room watching the **boring** news of the world. Just as I was about to get too bored, I saw a newscaster standing in front of Balloon.

"This brand-new restaurant Balloo has a pest of a problem. According to signs, it seems Balloo is serving up more than food: It's serving bugs. Leslie Eisenberg was there last night, so we asked her to tell us what she saw."

Leslie Eisenberg's head filled up the screen. "I didn't see a thing. At some point, people just started screaming and half the restaurant ran out."

"That's certainly not a very good sign," the newscaster said. "I know I won't be making reservations there any time soon. Ed, back to you."

And that is when my parents turned off the **TV** and looked at each other.

"Bugs!" my dad shouted, slapping his hand down on his knee. Then he turned to my mom.

"Bugs?" she asked.

They both looked straight into my eyeballs.

"Birdy, did you see any bugs at Balloo?" asked my dad. It was time for me to tell them.

"Yes, as a matter of fact. I did. I

was the one to tell Maria Cross all about the bugs."

Their **expressions** turned serious.

"What exactly do you mean?" my mom asked.

I told them all about seeing the bugs on the plate, and writing the note to Maria Cross, and how she read it and then everyone **ran** out of the restaurant. And also about how we put up all the signs that made it on the actual **boring** news of the world! I

didn't even take **a breath** until I was
finished speaking.

"What did these bugs look like,
exactly?" my dad asked.

"They had little heads popping out
of their shells."

And that's when I realized
something. And that something was
this: The bugs looked like snails.
Slimy, slippy, disgusting snails.

And revolting. I don't know why my brain didn't think of this sooner. Sometimes it forgets things when it gets too full.

But you will not even believe this. Instead of being proud of me for saving everyone's lives, they got upset! And then, the **worst** news of the world came down into my ears. You are not even going to believe this either.

They *were* snails.

And, you are not going to believe your ears about this next news: At French restaurants, PEOPLE EAT SNAILS! The **fancy** name for it is *escargot*.

"But how could we know that grown-ups like eating snails?"

"How about asking?" my dad asked.

I squinched my face at that one.

Asking! Elliott and I hadn't even thought of that. We just went right ahead and **assumed**. Assuming is when you think you know something without asking. Mostly, I have started to learn that when I assume things, I am usually wrong.

"Let's just go back and put a sign on the restaurant saying we were wrong," I suggested.

And that is when both my parents started to get really **frantical**. My dad was worried about the signs being up. My mom was worried about the story being on the news. My dad was worried about Maria Cross. My mom was worried about the restaurant. I could not even believe that mistaking snails for bugs would cause all this **worry**!

CHAPTER 12

"I'll drive into town and take down the signs," my dad said as he grabbed his car keys off the **coffee table**. "And when I get back, I'm going to call Elliott's parents to make sure they speak to Tenley, so that nothing like this happens again." My stomach dropped when I heard this. I hoped Elliott's parents wouldn't get too angrified with Tenley.

As my dad rushed out the door,

my mom rushed over to the computer. That's where she found out how to call the television station and also how to call Maria Cross! She called the news and told them the whole story. However and **nevertheless**, I had to call Maria Cross on my very own.

"How can I call her—I don't even know her?" I asked my mother.

I knew right away that I shouldn't have said this because of the way the breathing holes in my mother's nose got bigger and rounder.

"That certainly didn't stop you from sending her a note," my mother said in a talk-shout. "Now you have no choice but to deal with the consequences."

It is a scientific fact that I do not like to "deal with the consequences."

Consequences are the bad things that happen to you after you've done a bad thing.

I was very nervous and frightened about talking to Maria Cross. Grown-ups can be scary sometimes. Especially the kind you've never even met before.

I took the phone into my bedroom and closed my door because I needed to be **all by myself** when I called her. Otherwise I would get too nervous.

I opened my music box and took out a couple of jelly beans. After I finished them, I felt **ready** to call. The phone rang. The phone rang again. The third time it rang, it only rang half because someone picked up.

"Hello?" a woman's voice said.

"Hi. May I please speak to Maria Cross, the very famous restaurant reviewer?" I asked.

That is when the lady **giggled** and said, "Well, who may I say is calling?"

"This is Frannie B. Miller of Chester, New York. I am actually and nevertheless a food critic myself and I have some very important information to give her."

"Is that so?"

"It really is," I said.

"Well, you're in luck," the lady said, "because you're talking to Maria Cross."

I gasped. "Wow," I said.

"Wow, indeed," she responded. *Indeed* is a very **wonderful** word that grown-ups use that I need to **remember**. "So what's this very important information you have for me?"

"I'm the one who sent you the note at Balloon saying that the restaurant had bugs in the kitchen, but it turns out that they were not bugs at all. What they were, exactly, was SNAILS! My parents told

me that adults eat snails! So
I need to tell you that I was wrong.
There are no bugs at that Balloon
restaurant."

"Actually," said Maria, "snails,
like clams and squids, are mollusks,
not insects."

That was a word I had never heard
before. "They're mullets?" I asked.

This is when Maria Cross laughed
really hard out loud. I would have
laughed, too, but I didn't know what
was **so funny**.

"Mullets are really bad haircuts,"
she explained, and that's when,
instead of snails, I pictured a lot of
bad haircuts on a plate and laughed
out loud, too.

"About the note," she continued.
"I'm afraid it wasn't me you gave it to."

I was stumpified. "It wasn't?"

"No, I haven't been to Balloo yet. I'm going next Friday night."

"Oh," I said. "Then who did I give the note to?"

"I don't know, but I'm sure you gave her quite a scare."

"I did. She ran out of the restaurant screaming."

This made Maria laugh right out loud again.

"You are quite a character, Frannie B. Miller," Maria Cross said. Then she asked, "What else did you say in your review?"

"Well, I said that there was a waterfall in the bathroom and there were sprays that smelled like roses. I also said that I didn't know why they left the *n* off the word *Balloon*."

Then she laughed really out loud.

"Frannie, you sound like a lot of fun."

"I am," I said. But then I worried that that sounded too **braggish**, so I added, "At least, sometimes."

"Say, would you like to be my dinner companion next Friday night at Balloo? You could help me write my review, and I certainly would like to see the review you wrote."

I sucked in a fast **gulp** of happiness.

"Really?" I asked.

"Really," she said.

"Hang on and I'll go ask my mom."

Then I ran down the hall yelling in the most excitified way and she said **yes** and then I went back on the phone and I made grown-up plans with Maria Cross to review Balloon for the second time.

CHAPTER 13

My parents were still pretty angry at me and had some conditions about going back to Balloon. First, I had to **apologize** to the actual owner of Balloon before going back for another meal. Plus, I had to think of a way to *show* the owner I was sorry instead of just *saying* I was sorry. That was a really hard thing to figure out. THEN I had to write to the "Dear Editors" section in our local newspaper and tell **the real story** AGAIN of what happened. By the time I was done with all those sorrys, I was going to be foreverteen years old! At least I knew for a scientific fact that I would never ever do anything like this again!

I *also* had to be on my best behavior with Maria Cross and not give away the fact that she is **a reviewer**.

My parents decided they liked Balloon so much that they made a **reservation** for the same night, but they would sit at a different table, of course.

The really scary part was when I had to go to Balloon and apologize. We went on Thursday night. That way, it would not have been **illegal** for me to go back there the next day.

The owner was a very scary

French man. He did NOT think the story was funny at all. In fact, he was very serious and not only mad at me, but at my entire worldwide family. That gave me a very bad-day feeling in my **belly** because they didn't do anything wrong. He was red in the face and walked back and forth in front of us, throwing his hands **all over the place while he talked**. Finally, he ended by saying everything was okay, but . . .

"It was very embarrassing for us, you know."

I nodded my head because I did know.

I thought I knew how to make things better, actually, but I couldn't tell him because it was a secret. It had to do with Maria Cross. Which meant he

was going to have to **wait**. But he was
certainly going to be very surprised
by that sorry. The other sorrys I could
show him now. I turned around to my
dad, and he put the cookie jar filled
with all the **jelly beans** in my hands.
I turned around and handed them to
the red French man.

"I won this at my school fair
because I guessed almost the right
number of jelly beans. My parents
explained that I took something away
from you by saying you had bugs
when you didn't. That is why I decided
that I would take something away
from me and give it to you. Which is
why I would like you to have all the
jelly beans I've ever had in my entire
worldwide life."

That is when the red French man

made a **teeny** little smile out of the corner of his mouth. I'm really smart about teeny little **corner** smiles. He took the jelly beans from me and said, *"Merci beaucoup,"* which is how French people say "Thank you very much."

Then I turned around, and my mom handed me the poster that I made for him to hang on the front door. It was a picture of me that I drew with a big **cartoon** bubble coming out of my mouth that said:

I am Frannie B. Miller and there are no bugs at balloon. What they are exactly are SNAILS! I made a mistake and I am very sorry.

When he saw the poster, the other corner of his mouth gave a teeny little smile, too. I was starting to feel **better about everything**. Even snails!

Then he looked at my parents and smiled at them and said, "*Je suis très impressionné!*"

That is how you say "I am very impressed!" in French.

CHAPTER

Since I apologized to the owner
and he **accepted**, I was not afraid
to go back to Balloon on Friday
night. And you will never believe in
your worldwide life what I'm about
to tell you.

Maria Cross e-mailed my parents
to say she was going to wear a disguise
to Balloon! A for instance of what I
mean is that when famous restaurant
critics go to restaurants they sometimes

wear **wigs** and glasses and hats so no one recognizes them! The best part of it was that she said I could wear one, too!

I wore my **prettiest dress**, the blue one with the yellow flowers all over it. That part was not my disguise. But my dad's **old glasses** with the lenses taken out *were* part of my disguise. So were the **millionteen barrettes** in my hair. Also, I brought my briefcase: business cards, résumé, envelopes, pencils, and a broken remote control so the briefcase would feel heavy.

When we got to the restaurant, we saw a woman waiting outside. She was very tall with black hair that went past her chin and glasses. Her glasses were just like mine except they still had lenses in them! She didn't look anything like the wrong Maria Cross.

But I wanted to know what she looked like without the disguise.

"Maria, if that's a wig, then what's your real hair like?" I asked.

"Frannie!" my mother shouted. "That's not a very polite question!"

Maria laughed. "It's okay."

I was glad Maria said it was okay for me to ask. Because I really wanted to know.

"My hair is long and blond. And the glasses are fake, if you're wondering."

Once we were inside, my parents went to their own table and I sat down with Maria Cross. She asked me all sorts of questions, like: *Tell me more about yourself!* and *Would you like to order off the adult menu tonight?*

I did order off the adult menu. It was **the most fantastical dinner**

I've ever had. Not the food so much, but every other part. Maria gave me a piece of paper from her pad, and I got to write down all the words that came to my mind about the food. Then she explained the way she tasted food, and it was very interesting, but my tongue didn't taste anything *silky* or *tender.* It just tasted like carrot soup and boring old chicken.

The surprise of the night was that Maria ordered escargot! When they arrived they looked as **buggy** as they did before. I could not believe my worldwide eyes that she ate them. Then I could not even believe my eyes even more when she liked them.

"Part of a food critic's job is to try new things. How about you try a snail?" she asked, pushing the plate toward me. My stomach was very worried, but like I said earlier, I'm a very jobbish kind of person. If trying new things is part of the job, then I will **try new things**. She showed me the way to pull the snail out of its shell with a very **skinny** fork. Then I closed my eyes and held my nose from the inside and put the snail in my actual mouth! And then I chewed and you will not even believe this scientific fact: I liked it! Maria Cross was very proud of me for being so brave. I was proud of me, too. And, also, really surprised that my mouth liked the **snail taste**.

Then, at the best part—dessert— Maria Cross asked my parents to join us. You will not even believe it about the desserts. We ordered about **three hundred desserts** to share. The best was the slice of chocolate cake, which was as thick as eighty slices put together. And there was chocolate mousse inside of it! And inside of that? STRAWBERRIES! It was the best dessert I've ever had in my entire life as a person.

Then Maria Cross told me the most exciting things about restaurant reviews. You got to give out stars. Five stars is the very best and zero stars is the very worst. She asked how many stars I would give Balloon, and I told her I'd give it five. My new review would say that this restaurant was spectacular. Telling her how good I thought the restaurant was was my other way of showing my sorry.

At the end of the meal, we walked her to her car, and that was when she handed me something. It was a small piece of paper, and I looked at it. It had her name and number on it. It was her business card! I was so excitified, and that is when I remembered I had business cards, too! I opened my briefcase and took out a business card and handed it to Maria Cross. She put it right in her purse so it would never get lost.

"Don't forget to look at Wednesday's paper," she said as she got in her car. "You might find yourself in it!" And then she waved and drove away.

That night I got home and wrote my second review of the restaurant Balloon. I decided to leave the *n* off the name because Balloo is what the chef calls it and it's his restaurant. I wondered if Maria Cross said the same things in her review as I said in mine.

I could not wait to find out what she said. I also could not believe what a good restaurant reviewer I was turning out to be.

Maybe one day I'd even open my own restaurant. Elliott could stand in

the front where people would give him
their names, and I could be the main
waitress. Maria Cross could eat there
for free. I'd invite Mrs. Pellington and
I wouldn't drop one thing on her. I'd
even let the **red French man** work
there, if he wanted. My mom and dad
would have a regular table like we
have in the dining room at home. It
would be the coziest, best restaurant
ever. I already have a name for it:
Balloon. And you know what will be
the special of the night? Snails.

Balloo
by Maria Cross
4 and a half stars
Smack in the center of Chester, NY, sits a
brand-new French restaurant whose younger

patrons are confused by the missing *n* at the end of its name. Outside of that missing *n*, there's not much missing at Balloo. The toasted almond and beet salad was exquisite. The pairing of salt and sweet hit just the right notes. The Rosemary Chicken was silky and tender, and the Chocolate Mousse Cake with strawberries was the best I've ever had. The snails caused early alarm. Mistaken for insects by a budding young food critic, these snails even made it on the news. And well they should. They are newsworthy snails: the standout in a sea of standouts. I'd travel far to dine on Balloo's snails. And so should you. They are divine.

Balloo
by Frannie B. Miller
Grown-ups eat weird things
like seaweed and snails and
probably other things that come

from the bottom of the ocean
that I don't want to know
about. Last week I didn't know
that you could eat snails, but
now I do. That's because I
told the entire world of Chester,
new York, that Balloo, the new
restaurant with no n on the
end of its name, was serving
bugs. Really, they were snails
and I was wrong. That is a
for instance of why you should
eat at Balloo without worrying.
And also because I even ate
one and it tasted good. not as
good as the desserts, though.
The desserts are delicious and
there is nothing weird in them.
Thank you for reading this.

THE END.